KANE
RISING

KANE RISING

THE SIBLINGS OF KANE

by

JANETTE ANDERSON

BearManor Media

2012

Kane Rising: The Siblings of Kane
© 2012 Janette Anderson
Janette Anderson Entertainment
WGA West 1374532

For information, address:

BearManor Media
P. O. Box 71426
Albany, GA 31708

bearmanormedia.com

Typesetting and layout by John Teehan

Published in the USA by BearManor Fiction

ISBN—1-59393-382-7

Dedicated to
Gary Daniels

Chapter 1

Men, with faces tortured in pain, lay dying all around him. His men… his unit. The rescue chopper, with a bold red-cross sign emblazoned on the side, hovered above them ready to land on the scorched, rotting earth. From three sides the flames engulfed the old metallic bird, its body glistening in the flame-burned sky. Behind them…Viet Cong.

"Get those men inside that fucking piece of metal!" With nowhere to run, Sergeant Kane Branson turned, firing his well-worn M-15 until he emptied the rifle, and then flung the useless weapon to the ground. Reaching for his companion's means of fire, Kane stretched down, grabbing the gun from its resting place next to his number two.

Alex lay on the parched earth, blood pouring from his gaping chest wound. Kane raised the gun and fired, seemingly endless rounds, and the enemy fell to the ground. In slow motion, Branson gestured to his men to move, and he yelled at the top of his lungs.

"Everyone get into that chopper. Go, you stupid bastards!" Branson's deep, masculine voice echoed through the jungles of smoke and time.

He pulled the black bandana from his head, and bound it tightly round his own shattered arm. Blood dripped down what was left of his army shirt, reaching his scarred fingers, and dribbled to the ground, making red pools in the decaying earth.

"Sarge, save your self. Leave me!" Alex's voice could hardly be heard above the noise of war.

"The hell I will! You're too much of a bastard to die."

"Sarge, behind you!" screamed Alex, pointing with his one good arm. The other clutched the wound in his chest.

Kane turned with one swift movement and brought his hands up around the lone Vietnamese throat. The scrawny opponent hung in his grasp while Branson, with some difficulty, pulled a large knife from his belt, and, without hesitation, Kane Branson slit the captor's throat. Dropping the man to the blood-stained earth, he turned his attentions back to Alex.

Kane swung the spare gun over his shoulder, and bent down to get his comrade. His arms slid under Alex's, and, through his own pain, hoisted his friend to an upright position. In one maneuver, he raised him up and over his shoulder. Kane groaned under the dark-skinned man's weight, and ignoring his own pain that seared through his brain, began his seemingly long journey to the waiting craft. He could hear his men calling him and urging him to hurry as he trundled on through bloodied corpses lying in all positions on the ground. Branson's tired legs ached and his vision blurred, but still he kept going. Sweat ran down his forehead, mixing with filth and grime, ending up misting tortured eyes.

With one final burst of energy, he reached the waiting chopper. Black and white hands reached out and pulled their battered comrades inside the open doors. He made sure Alex went in first. Branson remembered someone grabbing his arms, pulling him to safety, and then the world as he knew it exploded. Time stood still, and brilliant, white light blinded him and he knew no more.

Kane came back to a harsh reality as thick, white snow took the place of his countless memories. Like his over-crammed mind, the crowded gravesite loomed into view as he watched limousine after limousine turn into the entrance of the cemetery. Kane pulled his coal-black leather jacket around him and he leaned forward astride the motorcycle seat to get a better view of the procession. It was a long time since he had been to the cemetery, thinking back to when his grandfather had been buried, and he had never seen a snow like today since then in this part of Australia. As he moved slightly on the long, sleek flying machine, Kane felt pain once more sear through his chest. Tight, crisp-white bandages over most of his upper torso restricted him from leaning as far as he needed to get the view he desired most. He slumped down on the body of the bike to find relief, resting his arms across the handlebars. Flakes of soft, new snow drifted onto his long, slightly-graying hair and he brushed them off with indifference. Pulling his collar up around his neck, Kane pushed the unruly hair inside the jacket and shivered.

It was cold, really cold. Icicles hung from the trees and snow lay in enormous piles along the cemetery path where plows had cleared the rugged driveway for today's military funeral. On the hill above the cemetery wall, the lone warrior sat draped in the sorrow of his young wife's death.

"Have you seen him? Do you think he is here? Surely-to-god he wouldn't stay away from his own wife's funeral?" Lord paused, mulling that thought over. "Would he?" Dan Lord's breath streaked out ahead of him in the frosty air and his tired eyes scoured the cemetery grounds, tired from the nights of minding all the children, his two and Kane and Kelly's. He couldn't see his father-in-law anywhere. Still he stood there waiting, always on duty.

"He's here!" Ex-Commander Buchanan frowned, but was confident in his statement. "You just can't see him. Commander Branson is here!" With salt and pepper hair, a face lined from years in the Australian police force, Buchanan knew his agent. Correction, he knew his boss. Kane was there. Buchanan turned 360 degrees, shivering in the afternoon cold, his thick, grey coat not offering him the protection he needed. He blew warmer air onto his gloved hands. Even thick lambs wool couldn't keep the frigid air out. Why wasn't Kane down there with them… with his children? He was still convalescing from the terrible ordeal in Iraq and his horrific injuries sustained from the knife wound made by Ryan Holden. That was where Kelly Branson died… by her own hand, thinking that Kane was dead. And Kane had thought he was dead, too, and how he had wished to God he was. This thought brought Buchanan back to reality and he turned to see the limo draw up carrying the siblings of Kane.

As the car door swung open, Sage Branson-Lord stepped out first, pregnant once more with Dan Lord's child. Kane's eldest daughter stood in the snow and looked up to the skies. It was a look that made Buchanan shudder, for he had seen it before many years ago on Kelly Branson's face when she thought her beloved husband, Kane, was dead. Now he saw it again. Sage stared at the grey sky as the flakes landed on her hair and eye lashes, finally resting on the long black coat she wore. There was a look about her that brought sadness to Buchanan.

"God damn the man! Is he always gonna treat his family like this?" muttered Buchanan, as he watched Sage, and then he waited for the apple of Kane's eye to emerge from the limo.

Sage turned back, reached her hand into the car and a tiny, gloved hand grasped hers. Star Branson emerged from the snow-covered limo. Dressed from head to toe in black, her long, blonde hair draped itself around her shoulders and hung there. Buchanan had never seen a more angelic child than Kane's young daughter. She was ten going on twenty. Star stood next to her half sister, Sage, and clung tightly to her hand. The pair stared ahead of them across the cemetery. It was obvious they were looking for their father, one who didn't want to be seen just yet.

From the other side of the limo, the driver opened the door. Gingerly, Kene Branson stepped out of the car and into the grownup world of misery and suffering. Behind him came Kip, the youngest Branson, his blonde hair tussled in the afternoon light. Immediately the two boys clasped hands as Dan Lord came round to shield the boys from harm. He ushered them to the front of the car to where his wife and his small sister-in-law stood. Star looked up at Dan, her father's closest friend and her protector, and her Branson blue eyes pleaded for the truth. Where was her father? Why wasn't he here with them?

As if sensing the feeling, Sage brought the thoughts to voice. "Where is he? Where is my… our father? Where is Kane?" Her voice faltered.

"Buchanan says he is here. Just not ready to face reality yet and show himself. Hopefully he will before the funeral is over." Dan answered her as if in some kind of trance. He couldn't take his eyes off Star. Somehow she looked different today.

"Don't you have his cell number? Can't you call him?" Sage stopped speaking. "No, of course you can't. He wouldn't answer. Kane is Kane. Our father will do what he wants to do." None-the-less giant tears suddenly spilled from her eyes and down her cheeks. She felt Star squeeze her hand. Suddenly the child had become the adult and also the comforter.

"Daddy knows we can be brave. Daddy always knows," Star's voice was confident and strong just like Kane wanted her to be. She was her father's favorite child and she knew it, taking the responsibility well. She continued. "He knows I... we love him. He always knows." It was then that something made Star look towards the embankment above the cemetery and she saw just a tiny glint of silver from the Harley's gas tank. Her eyes were round like silver dollars, and she peered harder at the specter. It glinted again, as Kane purposely turned the bike sideward, gas tank towards Star.

"Daddy!" she whispered so low that she could hardly be heard.

"What?" asked Dan, leaning towards her. "Where?" He turned sharply in the direction Star was looking and then back at her, setting his hands on her tiny shoulders. "Where is Kane?! You see him, don't you? He somehow let you see him, didn't he, just like he would let Kelly..." and he stopped dead and composed himself. "Star, I'm sorry... I..." and he released her, turning away ashamed of his outburst and exhibition of open jealousy of his sister-in-law. She was just a child, but a child that knew more about Kane than any other living person.

Star brushed the tears from her face with gloved fingers. She felt a rushing noise in her ears. For one brief second she saw her father and felt his presence, and then the connection was gone.

Kane felt it, too, as he saw his beloved Star. How he wanted to hold her right now, hug her and tell he loved her. He shook his head and tried to clear his mind, one that right now was in total confusion. When he saw Star, he saw Kelly. Maybe he had left the hospital too soon. Maybe he should have just ridden with them in the limo. Maybe... Kane leaned his head into his hands and openly wept.

Chapter 2

The old church in the cemetery was quaint by any standards. Today it was decorated with white roses, seemingly hundreds of them, some in full bloom and others quietly closed, still in bud. Dan Lord escorted his own wife, and Kane's family, down the aisle to the front of the church. Buchanan followed closely behind them along with other Federal personnel from the office. The Australian Federal Police were out in force. Not only roses adorned the church but agents, too, friends of the Commander and also friends of Kelly stood in the old wooden pews. In the isle near the back, waiting to take their seats, were people that Dan had never seen before, but one he very definitely knew. She caught his eye and nodded very slightly to him. Dan's thoughts were in turmoil as he recognized United States Marshal Reese Wade. Why was she here now? Hadn't Kane given up enough for her? Like some angel of death, had she come back to claim Kane for her own? Next to her stood a girl, maybe nine or ten years of age that sported long, dark-brown hair, and there was something oddly familiar about her. Dan kept going down the isle turning his head around to look at the age-old glass window that belonged to the far end of the church.

At the front of the church, the pastor waited with some anticipation for the congregation to settle. Kelly's coffin rested there, standing lonely, flowers almost covering the casket. No one stopped the procession of folks. No one dared to. Dan glanced up the front pew where a lone figure silently stood. Dan shuffled along the wooden seating till he reached the tall, blonde-haired Chinaman also dressed in black. His hair was in stark contrast to his features and his clothes, looking almost out of place on his head.

"Sam," and Dan extended his hand to Kane's forty-year-old son, Sam Branson.

"Dan. Where is Kane?" His tone was to the point and once again the Branson steely-blue eyes almost bored a hole through his brother-in-law.

"You don't know either? I thought, you of all people, would know. Or Star…" and Dan half turned towards her. Dan dropped his voice to a whisper. "Star knows. She just won't say, but she knows. Kane let her see him somehow."

"Where?" Sam questioned, glancing round the church, his eyes ever narrowing.

"Outside!" replied Dan, gesturing towards the door. "Not in here."

"Mr. Buchanan," and Sam once more extended his hand to the other agent, who reciprocated the gesture. "What was my father doing out of hospital anyway? Wasn't he supposed to be under supervision? I should have come back with him. I don't believe I didn't do that! It was stupid!"

"You didn't know he would leave the hospital. None of us did. Kane is Kane. He does what he wants to, always has and always will. I just wish he was here for the kid's sake. They need him…" and Dan hesitated and glanced towards the two little boys. "They are too young to fully understand that their mother is never coming back, but Star…"

"I think you underestimate Star. She is her father's daughter. They have a connection just like Kane had with Kelly… why, why didn't she check first before she pulled the trigger? If only she had… or one of us had stopped her. If only Hunter or I had…" Sam shook his head and his voice trailed off in disgust at himself.

"You can't blame yourself, Sam… it wasn't your fault. She thought he was dead. Hunter recounted everything. I was there at Kane's bedside when he told the story… and God forbid, he has to go through it again at the inquest. A federal agent can't just die. Her death has almost destroyed your father. He doesn't want to live, not without her." Dan paused, "I'm not sure even the children can save him… I'm sorry, I meant the young ones!" Dan felt like an idiot stating that to one of the siblings.

"I know what you meant and I think you may be right. I guess it depends if Kane shows in the church. We can only wait and see if he does." Sam looked down at Star. "I think you are right, Dan. Star is the only one that knows!"

It was as if Sam gave Star the cue. She slid past Dan and stood next to Sam, small, but defiant like her father.

"Our Daddy is here, Sam. I saw him outside on the hill." Star was so precise and so grown up for ten, as mature as Kane would want her to be.

"Are you sure? Could have been someone else there, you know, passing by." Sam looked down at her, questioning her, all the time knowing she was right.

"It was Daddy. He turned the bike so I could see him better. Should we go and get him? I can go…" and Star turned to leave the pew.

He placed his arm on her young shoulders. "No!" Sam's tone became more subtle. "Kane will come to us if he wants to. Sit here by me, Star…" and he spoke softly to her as the organ started to play and the tiny church was hushed from voices. No one had time to ask why Reese sat at the back of the church.

Soft strains of organ music filled the air outside the church. Kane was beginning to feel he could stay away no longer. He rose up on the Harley and started the machine, its voice like a death rattle between the cemetery walls. Kane's leather-gloved hands revved the throttle and the noise echoed through the snows of ancient times. Driving slowly down the icy track to the main entranceway, he hesitated on the motorcycle, picking his way through the high ridges on snow banks. Carving his own path down to the church gates, he waited, with engine purring, mainly to let everyone into the church that needed to be there. He noted the people going in, who showed up and the ones who didn't… Kane waited till he was ready to make his entrance. And make it he would…when he wanted to.

Kane parked the bike, kicked the stand into position, leaned against it and removed his gloves, one by one, laying them on his bike. From the back of his ever-tight, black jeans, he pulled out his traditional brand of cigarettes. He stared at the packet, thought deeply about smoking and decided against it. Perhaps this was not the right place nor was he in the right condition to smoke. He pushed them back into his jeans, replaced the gloves on his hands and proceeded down the path towards the entrance of the church. Kane didn't know how he was going to handle this. He missed Kelly so much. He loved Kelly so much... He could hear the organ inside grinding out music in the church, and could feel death surrounding him from all sides of the cemetery. In front of him stood closed doors, big oak things that looked formidable. Kane hesitated. He looked down at himself dressed in leather... black leather. He smiled. Kelly would appreciate that... god, why had she pulled that trigger? Why didn't she just wait till he was conscious? He couldn't speak, when on the ground, thinking he was dying as his chest sported a running river of blood; he couldn't tell her he was still alive. How he had tried to and how he had failed... and failure was not on his resume!

The light outside was fading. Kane looked up at the sky towards the winter sun. It offered him no comfort. He reached the doors and pulled them open; no one stopped him as he stepped inside, his black snakeskin boots echoing on the stark brick floor of the church causing folks to turn their heads. He unzipped his jacket and the crisp white shirt came open with it, revealing the seemingly endless reams of bandages underneath. His hair dropped out of its hiding place and cascaded down his shoulders. Kane stood there bathed in the lights from the church, a formidable foe and a warrior ready for battle, and as always packing a gun in the back of his jeans.

Reese Wade saw him first and she gasped, clutching her hand to her mouth. There was a sadness about him that she had never seen before. A haunting, disturbing look that she feared would never go away. Was this the same man she was still in love with? Perhaps now was not the right time or place? She pulled the child next to her even closer to her skirts. Now was certainly not the time...

Kane, as if sensing her presence, turned in Wade's direction. His electric-blue eyes switched on and staring, offering no hint of pleasure in seeing her there. It was her fault Kelly was dead. If only they had not been on the mission to rescue Wade in Iraq, his beloved Kelly would still be alive. All he had for Reese was contempt and it showed in his face. Reese cringed.

Kane turned his attentions to the front of the church as he heard a small voice.

"Daddy!" Star had heard the doors open and had seen her father enter. She knew he would come, Star always knew, just like Kelly had known. She pushed past Dan and her stepsister and rushed out into the aisle. Like the angel she was she walked slowly between the pews till she reached her father, sliding her hand into his, and she, too, looked across to Reese Wade and hate sprang from every pore at the woman who held the child to her.

"Daddy, why is *she* here?" Star asked of her father. She had never met Reese before, but somehow she knew who she was.

"Not sure, baby. Only know I don't want her here. Don't want her anywhere near us. If it wasn't for her, your mommy would still be alive..." Had he really said that out loud? He had, but he had meant it... and at that precise moment he hated Reese Wade.

Chapter 3

Kane stopped at the pew, and Star felt his hand tighten round hers. She looked up at her daddy's face. Star wasn't short like Kelly had been. She would be tall and blonde like Kane. Her back was straight and in her eyes there was a fire, just like there was in Kane's.

"What the fuck are you doing here?!" Kane yelled at Reese. He didn't give her a chance to answer. "We don't want you here and you are not welcome!" The 'we' meant him and Kelly? Or did it? "Go! Haven't you done enough? Kelly would still be alive if not for you!"

The organ music ground to a halt in a blur of tangled notes.

Hearing Kane's angry words, Sam rushed from his seat followed closely by Dan. They dashed down the aisle towards him. Sam was the first to reach his father.

"Kane, don't! This isn't the time or the place! Save it. This is your wife's funeral, for God's sake!" Sam reached for his father's leather jacket and he stretched his arm in front of him. "Kelly wouldn't want this… Kelly…" Sam stopped mainly because of the look in his father's eyes as he turned his head to stare at his eldest son.

"Kelly should not be dead. She should!" and he looked back at Reese, his face full of vengeance and his finger pointing maliciously at her.

"Kane! Stop it, you don't mean that and there are children here…" Sam begged him.

"Daddy knows. Daddy means it… just like I do… none of us want her here, Sam… Do you?" asked Star, her face contorted with hate and then the look was gone.

Sam was shocked. He didn't want Wade there, but he couldn't say it. He had noticed her on his way in just like Dan had, but now was not the time or place for a confrontation. Sam had not realized till now as he looked at Kane, how full of hate he was. He had changed so much in the last couple of weeks that Sam hardly knew the man he was holding on to… hardly knew his own father. "Kane, for the love of god, stop it, now!"

Kane looked down at Star, and then up to the front of church, and then back to Reese. "This isn't over, Reese! This will never be over between you and I, and I will never forgive you for coming here… never!"

"Kane!" yelled his son and the whole congregation turned to look at the man in the black leather. "Get a hold of yourself!"

Dan stepped in front of Kane, blocking him from doing anything violent in the House of God. But he had to admit he didn't want Reese there either. He half turned to look at her and there was the child again, long brown hair like Reese, but there was something only too familiar about her. He couldn't quite figure out what it was.

At the front of the church, Kene and Kip started to cry, gentle little sobs and then an explosion of sadness set in. They turned to Sage and clung to her legs not knowing quite why their father was yelling like some madman.

"It's ok, kids, shush. It will be okay. Our father is angry at someone at the back of the church. He will calm down…" 'Right,' thought Sage, 'the hell he will.' And in her mind she was just as angry at Reese Wade. Whatever she had to say to Kane it would keep. It was wrong of her to be there at Kelly's funeral. Sage glanced sideward at the coffin sitting there. She missed Kelly so much and had never had the chance to say goodbye to her. Sage and Kelly were more than friends; they were soul mates through Kane. They shared Kane, one was the daughter and one was the wife. She looked back down the isle at her father who was still red-faced and angry.

Kane realized that the whole church was staring at him. Sam was right. This was not the place. He leaned forward as far as Sam's reach would allow him to do and glared at Dan like he could see straight through him. "Reese... get out of here and take *your* child with you, now!" The emphasis was on *your* and more than one person noticed it.

Reese Wade stepped out into the isle pulling the child with her. The little girl looked fearful of the man yelling at her mother and clung to her skirts. She was quite the opposite of Star who, although still holding her father's hand, was as dominant as her father.

"Kane, I just wanted to pay my respects to Kelly and to your family... I..." she didn't say anymore. Her American accent was sour music to Kane's ears and she knew it. She couldn't even stand her ground against him... once, yes, but not now. "I'll leave." She dipped her head slightly and her long, brown hair almost touched her child. Reese was used to rebuffs from Kane but not quite like this. She tried to pass him and Dan but Kane stood in front of her.

He leaned just slightly towards her face. "You all but killed her. You knew right from the start it was Kelly that was on my mind and always will be... even in death!" Kane almost spat the words at her and his eyes were deep dark pools of despair and grief... like nothing Reese had ever seen.

"Kane... I am sorry. I never meant anything..." she tried to speak to him.

"That's right! You never did mean anything to me and you never will." He said the last statement so low that only she heard him, but he got the meaning over to her just the same.

She looked up at him then knowing it was probably the last time she would ever see him and she wanted to die. She had loved Kane for so long that she could not let go, and in that second she felt her heart shrivel and turn black... and vengeance entered the vacant space. Reese ushered the child down the aisle towards the doors. She glanced back once more to see Kane still staring at her, accusing her with his eyes, and Dan still stopping Kane from coming after her. Sam stood next to his father, tall and just as arrogant as Kane. No doubt in anyone's mind whose son he was. Reese felt the child pull on her skirt...

"Doesn't he like you?" the little voice whispered.

Before Reese could answer her child, the offspring spoke again, her bright blue eyes pleading for an answer.

"Mommy, I don't think my daddy wants to know me..." and her voice trailed off as she, too, glanced back at Kane, and the small child edged her way to the large oak doors and stepped out into the icy, winter snow, and the doors gently closed behind her.

Kane turned his head and his body towards the front of the church. His comments to Reese had been a warning and more than one person had heard it.

Star gripped her father's hand even tighter and she pulled him just a little forward in her direction.

"You can let go of me now," and Kane pulled in Sam's grasp and stared at his son.

"You sure? You remember where you are, right?" Sam confronted his father, slightly more than annoyed at him for such an outburst.

"Yeah, I know where we are. Somewhere we shouldn't be..." and he looked down at Star, and stopped speaking before he could utter more words of disrespect in the House of God than he had already.

Kane's eyes still squinted in anger and he was trying hard now to control his feelings. He pushed his hair back with his free hand, and then realized his shirt exposed a foot of chest covered in bandages, something he would rather his daughter had not seen. He pulled his shirt across him and tried to do up the buttons single-handed. He failed. Not wanting to let go of Star's hand, he pulled the jacket across himself instead. Sam stepped a little more towards him and slid the belt round for him so that his chest was now covered.

"Thanks," muttered Kane and looked into his son's face.

Sam's skin was lighter, like his Asiatic mother, Kane's lover, and Sam was clean shaven, whereas Kane still sported facial growth. His moustache and very slight beard were still blonde, unusual for a man turning sixty. Only his long hair was slightly graying. But the resemblance between father and son was apparent both in their arrogance, their build and hair color.

Kane was aware the whole congregation was still staring at him and at the front of the church his two little boys were crying their eyes out. They were too young at three years and five years of age to be grieving for the loss of their mother.

Seeing the look on Kane's face, Sam took control of the situation.

"Come on, Kane. Let's go get the kids. They need you right now," and Sam inclined his head slightly towards his step-brothers.

Kane's anger then switched down a notch or two. "Right, yeah, let's collect them," and taking the apple of his eye with him, Kane moved one heavy foot at a time to the front of the church.

Sam stepped aside and both he and Dan followed behind Kane till they reached the allotted seating where his other children sat. Kane inched his way along the pew till his sons and daughter could join him.

"Dad," and a very tearful Sage reached forward and put her arms round him. She was careful not to hold him too tight, and she felt him recoil just slightly from her hug. She looked into his face and she, too, hardly recognized the man in front of her. Was this really the same man from a few weeks ago? One who had moved heaven and hell to find his wife and now looked like he was entering the latter? Her thoughts were disturbed as Kane's two youngest boys vied for their father's attention. She chastised them slightly as she looked down at the two tiny Branson clones. "Your daddy can't pick you up right now, next week maybe…" and Sage wondered if there would be a next week for Kane and his family.

Kane let go of Star's hand and sat down on the old wooden pew. He wanted to lift both the boys up at one go and knew he could not. He touched them gently on their blonde mops of hair that each sported and ruffled them with his fingers.

"Hey, guys… no crying. Daddy's just fine. I am here with you now, and Star and Sage are here." As he spoke, Sam joined them and sat down next to his father. Kane looked towards his eldest son. "Sit on your brother's lap, Kip." He turned slightly to Sam. "Can you lift him up? I can't right now…" and under his breath Kane whispered, "I can't even lift a three year old child… dear god what has happened to me! I am a fucking invalid."

Sage heard him and wondered if 'Daddy' would ever be fine again!

Kane looked towards the alter and there he saw Kelly's coffin sitting quietly, waiting. It was the first time he had actually looked at it properly. It sat there adorned in flowers of all descriptions. Behind it stood a heart-shaped arrangement of white roses that he had picked out and next to that an oversized picture of Kelly in her AFP uniform mounted on a rather old looking easel. Kane stared at it. No one had asked him if this was okay to do… and he was the Commander, he would have said no! Probably that's why they had not asked him. This was, after all, a police funeral and he needed to remember that; also, he was the head of that establishment, and right now he was not setting the best example to the rest of the department. But Kelly's death had struck him harder than any physical damage could do. Kane didn't want to go on and that was obvious to everyone there. Kelly was the one who brought him back to life after his first wife's death. Kelly was there when his first love, Sam's mother, died in his arms. Kelly had given him three children. Kelly was always there… and now she was gone.

Kane felt a hand on his. Star reached for her father's sleeve and then his hand and she slipped it firmly into his, her fingers lost in his hand. Gently she squeezed in between her brothers and sat down by her father. It was if she read his mind.

"You have to go on, Daddy. Mommy would want that. You have to be strong for the little ones."

Little ones… she was just a little one herself. But somehow in those few moments, Star had taken over where Kelly left off. She would look out for Kane just like Kelly had done.

Sam looked from Star to Kane. The connection was there, one he would never share with Kane, but somehow he had to make it happen. Sam knew right there that Star could help Kane, and he, too, had to help his father another way. He would stay in Australia. It was more important than his life back home. If he had to bring his girlfriend and their child over to live in Australia, then he would do that. He knew that his father needed him. Sam had seen the look in Kane's eyes, one of a man who would become reckless to the point of abandonment and that Sam could never allow, and apparently neither would Star.

Chapter 4

Kane could see the pastor quite clearly as he proceeded gingerly with the service. He could hear every word that was said about Kelly, especially when Sage got up to speak about the personal side of her life and when Buchanan spoke about Kelly's time in the AFP. And then it was his youngest daughter's turn to say something about her mommy. Star stood up and let go of her Daddy's hand. She walked on up to the solid oak coffin and stood beside it instead of the alter steps. And Kane could hear her…

"And Mommy would want us all to go on and to grow up to be good people, because mommy was good people. Mommy told me how she met daddy." She looked directly at Kane. "Daddy thinks we don't know, but we do… and we are glad, because you saved mommy and she loved you so much…" and it was then Star faltered in her speech that she had obviously taken time to think about. "Mommy…" and she could not continue. Her eyes welled with tears and her mouth quivered.

Kane realized how selfish he had been. All he had thought about was his own grief. He rushed past his other children, into the isle and to Star's side. She slipped her hand again into his and side by side they stood, father and daughter totally united in a very special love for Kelly.

"What my daughter means," and Kane hesitated briefly, "is that we all will miss her terribly, but Kelly…" and he stopped again as he mentioned her name, "Kelly will always be in our hearts," and if driving the point home even more, "and for me, she will be the only woman in my life now and forever. I will pick up where my wife left off, being the parent to all my children. I will be here for them. Time to stop being the hero, time to perhaps retire…" He let go of Star.

The uneasy silence in the church was broken as murmurs rippled through the ranks of the AFP.

Kane continued. "We shall see, but for now, we go on, day to day…" He stopped and turned to the heart of roses. Picking the fullest blooming rose he could find, he pulled it from the wreath and laid it on the top of the coffin. "Kelly," he spoke softly then, bending his head just slightly. "I will always love you… No one will ever take your place," and he rested his hand on the coffin's side.

Tears flowed from his eyes and the force had never seen this side of the Commander before. Only Sam was not shocked at Kane's actions. He had seen Kane and Kelly in Lantau and Iraq and how close they were. Kane could take no more and he turned on his heel and with his boots clanging on the stone floor, he marched down the isle and out of the now open doors. No one stopped him. No one dared. He was Kane. Slowly, one by one, the mourners followed behind him. Star first, and then Sage, and Dan ushered the 'little ones' behind him. Sam followed with Buchanan.

"Is your father okay?" Even Buchanan who had known Kane for a century or so was worried and he watched Kane leave the church.

"Give him time… give him time. Perhaps for now you might want to put the deputy-commander in charge… just till this is over. A few weeks or so…" Sam didn't finish

"Maybe you are right… And what will you do, Sam?" Buchanan stopped in the isle, and he and Sam stepped to one side.

"Stay over here. Close the house up overseas and bring my girlfriend and new baby here. Maybe stay at the house with them all…" Sam looked Buchanan in the face.

"Keep an eye on him. Is that what you mean?" Buchanan could see more of Kane in Sam every time he looked at him.

"I guess that's what I mean. Something to think about." Sam hadn't thought about it till then. Now he was sure that's what he had to do. He should not have gone home and left his father in Australia.

Buchanan could see the distress on Sam Branson's face. "It wasn't your fault, Sam. You had no idea what was going to happen." Seeing the reaction on the younger man's face he changed the subject. "You can work with us again, you know like before. Work with Dan and the department. I can talk them into giving you a job for however long it takes for… well, you know what I mean." Suddenly Buchanan looked old. Retired officially from the force, but still with connections, he could make things happen. Getting Sam a job with them would be easy.

"Thanks. I would appreciate that. There is plenty of room at Kane's house, and if he doesn't want that I can get an apartment somewhere close to him." Sam kicked the snow with his boots.

Buchanan noticed Sam's boots were similar to Kane's. "You are at the house now though, right?" asked Buchanan.

"No. Took a hotel for last night. Will see how things lie later today. Sometimes… well, sometimes I still feel like the outsider not knowing my father till I was thirty-five. It was a shock for us all. Especially him." Sam dropped his head a little and his voice. His accent was more English than anything else having been raised in the best schools his mother could find for him. Lilia had spared no expense to raise hers and Kane's son.

"He thinks the world of you, Sam. You were all he talked about when he came back from Hong Kong. He may not have loved your mother like he should, but he would have done the right thing by her. You know that, and you know he loves you."

"I do know that. That's something I don't doubt from him…" and his words were lost in the crowd as the mourners moved on down the church aisle.

Both men moved out into the snow. Sam looked around for Sage and Dan. He wanted to help with his step-brothers. He saw his father's Harley sitting ready, waiting. 'Typical Kane,' thought Sam and he smiled. It was then he caught sight of a shadow in the early evening light. Snow flakes rained down enough to cause shadows in the air. Sam looked again, straining his eyes to see clearly. He blinked and blinked again. It couldn't be. He must be seeing things.

"Buchanan, do you see someone over there by Kane's Harley?" Sam was visibly shaken and it showed as he turned to ask Buchanan the question.

"Where?" asked a confused Buchanan and he, too, looked towards the motorcycle which now had a smattering of snow covering it.

"Right there, next to the Harley…" and when Sam looked back there was no one anywhere near it. "My mistake… got too much on my mind. Where's Kane?"

"Over there with the boys." Buchanan stopped speaking. "Sam," he hesitated again. "Look at Kane's face. He is staring straight at the Harley like you were. He looks like he's seen a ghost." The older man looked back at Sam. "Son, you okay?" asked the ex-commander trying to see what Sam had seen, but failing. "Sam, where are you go…" and he was talking to thin air.

Sam took off with great speed across the snowy path to where Kane stood.

"Dad… Kane…" Sam approached his father with some caution simply because of the astounded expression on Kane's face.

Kane looked at his son, or more through him.

"You saw something, didn't you?" asked Sam, hoping he wasn't going to be jumped on by Kane.

"Am I going insane? Am I?" Kane felt he was losing his reasoning. "I was looking at the Harley. Something made me look that way and I thought…" He paused. "I thought I saw Kelly!" and Kane looked at Sam like he was coming unglued.

"No, Kane. You are not going insane. What…" and Sam shook his head from side to side, "or who did we see… because I saw something, too."

"You did? Really? Let's walk over there…" and Kane left Sam standing with the boys.

Sam took off after his father and was only a few steps behind him. Perhaps he did have a connection with his father after all.

As they approached the Harley, the snow ceased just a little, and both men looked down at the seat. On the back of the leather the snow had been cleared, almost brushed away like someone had been sitting there, and on the handlebars hung a silver K on a chain. Kane reached into his shirt and pulled out his matching K, holding it between his fingers. This one was his. The one hanging there gathering snow was Kelly's.

Chapter 5

Kane grasped his chest. Pain shot through his heart and he leaned forward to gain support from the Harley.

"Kane! Are you okay? Dad…" and Sam grabbed Kane by the shoulders. "Say something… Kane!" Sam wasn't quite sure what was happening. He only knew that Kane was in misery. "Let me get Dan…"

"No! I'm fine. Just the stitches…" and Kane's breathing was labored. His face was lined with pain and Kane knew he was having yet another small heart attack. He also knew what he had seen. "Pocket," he muttered to Sam.

"What?" Sam was trying hard to hear him and make sense of this, leaning closer to hear what Kane was saying to him.

"Inside pocket… leather jacket…" Was all Kane could utter.

Sam reached his hand inside the jacket and found a small gold tin. He pulled it out, opened it, revealing pills. "This? Is this what you want?"

Kane nodded, reached for the tin and grabbed one pill. He slid it into his mouth. The lines on his face relaxed a little and once more he could breathe. "Thanks."

"How long has this been going on?" Sam knew a heart attack, however small, when he saw one.

"Since Stratton shot me in Malibu. I had a very small heart attack when I pulled the plug in the hospital …"

"When you what!?" Sam looked incredulously at Kane.

"Pulled the plug in ER so that Kelly would think I was dead and she'd get married again… something like that, anyway." His breathing became more controlled and Kane straightened up and looked his son in the face.

"You are insane if you thought that. Kelly would never have left you. She proved that…" and Sam stopped speaking. Bad timing for that statement. "Kane. Kelly is dead. You do know that don't you…" Who was he trying to convince? Himself of Kane? Someone wanted Kane to think Kelly was still alive. Or at least make sure Kane worried enough to the point that he would become unsure of himself. Kane was too sane for that… normally. But right now Sam thought maybe they might succeed.

"Yes, I know… she died lying across me… how can I not know, but someone wants me to think otherwise." Kane stopped speaking and lifted Kelly's silver K off the handlebars, realizing his gloves were gone. He had left them on the motorcycle and now they were nowhere in sight. Someone had taken those and put the K in their place.

"How are you feeling now? You fit enough to join them down at the gravesite? They are going to think something is wrong if you don't go back down. Buchanan's already wondering what the heck is going on, and the kids need you. I'll be with you the whole way. I am not going to leave your side, and judging by the way Star is watching you, neither is she. You are stuck with your siblings, Kane, whether you like it or not."

Kane had never felt the need for anyone except Kelly, but now he needed his son and his daughter, needed the comfort they could bring him. If he gave up now, he was letting them and Kelly down. So he would go on. He straightened his clothes, brushed the snow from his jacket, put his arm on Sam's shoulder and together they walked slowly back down to the gravesite and the waiting party.

As they went, Sam felt he had to know something. "Does anyone else know about *your* little secret? This one anyway…" He continued. "You know… Buchanan," Sam hesitated. "Dan…" and he went for the kill. "Star?"

"You think I would tell a ten-year-old child?" Kane cut his eyes sideward towards to his son. That wasn't the question Kane thought Sam was going to ask him.

"Star is ten only in years. In the real world she is eighteen or so. She knows, doesn't she? When did you tell her? Before Iraq?" asked Sam, knowing exactly what the answer was.

"You seem to know all the right questions... and the answers. Yeah, she knows and yes, before Iraq. And before you ask that's the only thing she knew." Kane was daring his son to ask about the heroin and the trip to Japan. "Star knows what I want her to know. One day when she's older, I will tell her the rest. Not now."

"You underestimate your daughter, Kane. She knows you better than you think. Remember that she's *your* daughter..."

"What the fuck does that mean," and Kane pulled away from Sam. "She's my daughter, for Christ's sake... .and she's ten! But it's hard to look at her and not see Kelly, if that's what you mean." He breathed deeply. Still a little short of breath but managing.

"That's what I mean..." Sam thought that's what he meant, and his thoughts were interrupted as they were joined by the young lady herself.

"Daddy, why did you go to your Harley? If you were looking for your gloves, I have them here." She was so precise and handed them to Kane.

"You have them, Star?" He questioned her. "When you were there, did you see anything else on the bike?"

"No, Daddy. Why?" She looked up and into his eyes. She really didn't know what he meant. "Should I have seen something else?" She brushed snow from her hair and shook her head making her hair fly out just a little. She stood way over four feet, and one day she would be up to Kane's shoulder, and Sam was right. Star did look like Kelly peppered with Kane's arrogance.

Sam could not help notice the change in Star since he had seen her last. In just a few months, she was a different girl. He had been told that she had spent a lot of time at the hospital with her father and the bond that was already there had grown even stronger than before.

"Daddy, are you feeling better now?" Star didn't even hesitate to ask him. "Did you find Mommy's K? The nurse gave it me to keep for you."

It was Kane's turn to look surprised. "How did you know..." And there was that feeling again like the one with Kelly. Maybe that's who he had seen by the Harley, Star getting the gloves. He tried to convince himself of that fact and failed miserably. But maybe he could convince Sam it was Star. "I'm just fine, baby. Just fine. Thank you for keeping the K for me." Kane turned to his son. "I guess it was Star we saw, Sam... what do you think?"

"Right, maybe. Could have been." And Sam, too, was totally unconvinced, but if Kane wanted to think that, then fine.

Sage appeared next to her father and slipped her arm into his. "Everyone is by the gravesite. Just waiting for you, dad. Ready?"

"As I will ever be." Kane paused. "When this is done, I need to go for a ride..." He stopped, mainly because Sage was looking at him like he was crazy.

"In this weather? Are you nuts?" Sage stopped speaking and saw the look on Sam's face and his head shaking very slightly side to side. "Whatever you want, Kane. Dan and I can take the kids home..."

"You take the boys. Star will ride home with me. There is something I need to show her."

"Kane, that's not the best idea," Sam intervened.

"I know what I am doing, Sam. Trust me. We won't be long. And Sam, make sure no one follows us." Kane pulled the gloves on. Even he was beginning to feel the cold. Black leather and shirt may be macho, but it wasn't very practical in this weather.

Sam figured Kane needed some space for just him and Star. And when he said no one, he meant the family and he also meant Reese Wade. There had been no sign of her outside and Kane had not mentioned her name again since the incident inside the church. But he knew his father had not and would not forget what had happened. And then a thought struck him. The little girl in the church, she reminded him of someone. Take away the brown hair, change it to blonde... my god... the child could be Star's sister! Sam had very clearly heard *your* child come out of Kane's mouth to Reese. Was that where he and Star were going now? Couldn't be, not after the way he had treated Reese. And how would Kane know where she was? Maybe he should just ask Kane? And maybe he shouldn't.

Chapter 6

He glanced at his father. There was nothing on his face to give anything away. Whatever Kane was thinking, they would find out later.

At Kelly's gravesite they waited as the coffin was solemnly lowered into the deep, snow sodden earth. His two small sons stood in front of Kane, his daughters stood one on each side of him. Sam stood next to Dan, who was right behind Sage.

"You have any idea what Kane is up to?" whispered Dan hoping to hide his voice behind his gloved hand. He looked so tired and his once dark hair was starting to grey prematurely. A little weight on him wasn't a bad thing, but wasn't too complimentary to his height.

"I have no idea." It was then Sam shared his thoughts with Dan. "You also wondered where Reese went?"

"What made you think…," Dan stopped speaking and looked at his brother-in-law. "Yeah. I wondered if that's where Kane is going. But how on earth would he know where to look and why would he take Star with him?" Good questions and ones that could not be answered. Only Kane could answer them. Dan turned his head and looked at his father-in-law.

Kane was the most ferocious, single-minded man Dan had even known. He had great respect for Kane and had worked under him and with him for years on the force. He knew that Kane would kill anyone in his way as he had done with the ruthless terrorist Ryan Holden, who had kidnapped Kelly and Reese Wade… not so much killed, but dismembered him. He cut out his heart. Dan shuddered. Kane was a killer, always had been and always would be… a killer with a license.

He watched him now, albeit from the side. Kane was everything Dan had wanted to be. Commander of the AFP, nice house… house… it was a mansion… money, respect, looks, build, power and most of all, Kelly… no, he didn't have Kelly. Kelly was the chink in his suit of armor. And now one of the links was missing and Kane would once more become the person he had been before Kelly. Smoking, drinking to excess, risk taker. And Dan had the feeling that Kane would no longer play by AFP rules. Now he had nothing to lose but his life.

And his children.

Dan turned his attentions to Star. Today she looked like a mini Kelly. He knew that Kane saw that, too. They were not father and daughter. They were sole mates. Sam disturbed Dan's thoughts.

"Is that who I think it is standing by the church door?" Sam squinted in the fading light.

"My god! It's Hunter. What is he doing here… now? Wasn't he away on an assignment for Kane?" And the penny dropped. That assignment included Reese Wade.

"Yeah, he was, and I think both you and I know what that was." Sam peered at Hunter, as the drone of the pastor's words continued. Sam didn't know quite what to do. He glanced at Kane, who was staring at the coffin like Kelly was about to rise up from it.

As if on cue Kane looked up and he, too, saw Hunter. His expression changed. He acknowledged Hunter with a slight nod of his head and then he looked back down as the coffin moved into its final resting place. Kane reached his hand across to Sage, and she took it willingly, grasping his hand almost frightened… she was losing her father. With his other arm he encircled Star to him, his arm resting lightly on her shoulders. His young sons clung to his legs almost unaware that that was their mommy down there in the dark, wet earth. Kane was getting the comfort from the children that he needed. His eyes were moist and at last Kelly was laid to rest. Kane could hear everything and he could see the service, but he wasn't really there. This had to be a dream… no, a nightmare. Then he heard the guns, the salute of firepower from the AFP for one of their own. He could see the Australian flag, folded, seemingly gliding towards him, carried by one of his own officers. He released his grip on his children and received the flag from Kelly's coffin. It was then he turned to Sam, the oldest sibling and handed it to him.

Sam looked shocked, but duly took it from his father's outstretched arms.

"Kane, I can't take this…" he choked on his own words.

"It's just a loan. Take it home for me. You will be there when I get back, won't you? I need you, Sam… I won't be long." Kane couldn't do this anymore. It was too much even for a killer. He tuned back to Star. "Ready?"

And Star spoke words she had never spoken before. "Yes, Kane."

It was then that Kane took one last look at the infernal manmade resting place of death. He closed his eyes and for one brief second he thought he felt a hand on his cheek and a light flutter of a butterfly wing on his lips. A sweet smell surrounded him and he could feel Kelly there with him like he had never felt her before. He whispered her name on the crisp evening air knowing this was the last time he would see her. He wanted the moment to last forever and he knew it could not. "Kelly, I love you, I always will… and whatever happens, baby, forgive me."

Sam heard the words and he didn't quite understand the last part of the sentence. He looked at Dan, who shrugged his shoulders. He had no answers for Kane's first born.

Kane opened his eyes. He still could not believe Kelly was gone. But what was more than true he didn't believe she was gone. It just would not sink into his brain. There had to be another reason she wasn't there. And that's where he and Star were going now… to find out the truth. And find it he would. He didn't look at the flag again and he didn't even glance at his own police department. He didn't want sympathy. He wanted justice. He didn't know what he wanted except to get Kelly back. Suddenly he realized he wasn't thinking straight. He shook his head from side to side and glanced at Sam and then to Dan. There were blank looks on their faces and he turned his attentions to his small sons.

"Sage, will you look after the boys. I promise I will be back soon… just some things to do." Kane didn't even glance at her, knowing that her look would be one of disgust for his ways. "Star, let's go… we have a place to be." Kane turned away from his family towards Hunter.

Hunter McLeod was Kane's trusted friend, bodyguard and deputy at the AFP. With coal-colored skin, the dark-haired, forty-old-year-old man had been with Kane in Iraq when he found Kelly. He had seen first hand what drove Kane to be the man he was, and Hunter admired him for that. He also knew that Sam didn't like him too much, mainly because his preference was not women, but to Kane that didn't matter... only that he would trust Hunter with his life and had already done so. Hunter pulled his long hair back into a ponytail and turned his boot-length coat's collar up around his neck. He wasn't wearing the AFP uniform today and didn't plan on doing that anytime soon. He, like Kane, was kind of a renegade, and that's what Kane liked about him the most... that, and the fact that whenever Kane needed him he was there.

"Gentleman," interrupted Hunter as he moved through the snow closer to his boss. Hunter nodded his head slightly to Sam and to Dan. "Mrs. Lord," his breath streaming ahead of him on the air and Hunter bent slightly to her. His attentions switched to Kane. "Commander, my motorcycle is right behind the church. I will follow you..."

Sam jumped in, touching his father's shoulder. "You said you didn't want to be followed, Kane..." his expression fierce as he took a step towards Hunter.

"I am sure that meant by you *blokes*," Hunter was curt to Sam. He faced Kane. "Ready, sir?"

"Yep, let's go." Kane didn't look at his son, just took Star's hand in his and ushered her away to the Harley without looking back... with Hunter right behind him.

Reaching the Harley, Kane climbed on first, Star right behind him. She nestled in to his back just like Kelly used to do, and wrapped her arms as far round him as she could, looking like she had been doing this for years.

Dan stared at his father-in-law. "What the hell was that about..." he chimed in. "He didn't even say goodbye to the people that came here..."

"That's the point, Dan. He couldn't... that would mean all this was final. He can't accept she is dead. And more importantly, how does Hunter know where to follow him to? There is something yet again that we are not part of." Sam stopped speaking. Something was very wrong with this picture. He wasn't sure what right now, but something was and he intended to find out just what.

Even with the inclement weather Kane sped off at the usual Branson speed of one to eighty in as many seconds. The speed didn't even faze his daughter. She rode on the back of the bike, her face turned sideward on her father's leather jacket, almost glaring at the men standing there staring at her. Shades of Kelly.

Chapter 7

"What the hell is going on, Sam?" I feel like we have been here before. Well, me, anyway. He left the whole family, except for Star. Have you any clue why Hunter was here hiding in the shadows as usual?" Dan was a little more than angry, and his voice was raised. This time Kane had shown disrespect to them all.

"Dan, it's ok..." Sage tried to stop her husband from saying more. "My father has to do what he wants. That's the only way he can function." And then she turned to Sam. "But he should have taken you with him, not Star. She's a child..." Sage paused, almost a little jealous of her sister. "No, I guess she isn't, is she?" as she watched Sam shaking his head.

"Let them go. Hunter will look after Kane. That's his job. He's Kane's bodyguard." Sam stated with some knowledge.

"His what? I thought that was done with in Iraq. Wasn't it done with?" asked Dan shaking his head, a little confused by Sam's last statement.

"I don't think it was. There is something going on that neither you nor I know about. But I intend to find out when Kane comes home tonight. Bad timing for questions or not! More importantly, where did they go? Hunter obviously came to the church for a purpose. And why was Reese here and why, in god's name, did Kane treat her so badly?" Sam pulled his cigarettes from the pocket of his coat. They were the same kind his father always smoked. While his sister carried on speaking, Sam slid a cigarette from the packet, and lit it up. Maybe not the right time to smoke, but like his father, he needed one.

"You wanted her here?" asked Dan, not bothering to be quiet.

"Hell no, but I wouldn't have thrown her out of the church quite like Kane did. Would you?" replied Sam at the same time blowing smoke out into the cold air.

"No, I guess not." Dan paused. "Strange, Hunter showed up right after Reese left, or was he waiting outside the whole time? Like on some sort of orders from Kane?"

"I think he was waiting and watched her go. I was wondering if he spoke to her, maybe found out where she was going." Sam was trying to put the pieces together.

"Probably. That would make sense. But why would he lead Kane to her and how would Kane know she would show up?" Dan could not figure this out. It wasn't like his father-in-law.

Both men looked puzzled. It didn't make sense.

"I hate to bring this up," and Sage paused, pulling her coat tighter round as she spoke. "Did anyone notice something familiar about the child with Reese?"

Time stopped. So now they had all seen it.

Sam broke the silence. "Yeah. The child looked like our father! Kane said they never…" and he looked down at Kene and Kip who seemed to be taking in every word that was being said, "You know… together… were they?" asked the older Branson.

"Not that I know of, and I was there the whole time right up till Dad *killed* Reese. He never saw her again, that we know of, till Iraq." She pulled the coat tighter round her body. "Dad wouldn't lie about that, would he? Tell me he didn't. That would mean that while he and Kelly were together, he…" Sage was visibly upset, her face screwed up in anguish.

"No! I am sure it's just coincidence. Lots of those today… but the child looked a lot like Star with dark hair, and I think Star saw it, too. That's why she was as hostile as Kane towards Reese, and, also why Kane took her with him. Some ends need tying up for him." Sam finished the cigarette and stomped it out under his boot.

Dan had seen Kane do that many times before. Sam was very definitely a Branson. Dan couldn't help think what an odd family it was. Sam, forty, Sage twenty-nine, Star was ten and Kene and Kip under five. That made him shudder. Kane didn't seem to know when to quit having kids… or at least who with. He shook his head. Had he really thought that and looked at the others to see if he had actually said it out loud. Apparently he hadn't. After being Kane's partner for so long, Dan felt he should have known Kane better than he did, but right now he wasn't sure he knew him at all.

"Dan… are you still with us?" Sam asked. "You putting pieces of the puzzle together or something?"

Dan looked startled. "Yeah, how did you know?" he asked him, thinking that Sam was as bright as Kane was.

"By your expression… and because it's what we do." Sam pulled Dan to one side, leaving Sage to cope with both the younger children, who were now clinging to their aunt.

"He didn't sleep with Reese, if that's what you are thinking. My father might be a lot of things, but not an adulterer!" retorted Sam.

"Right! He had sex with Corey on the way to rescue Kelly…" chimed in Dan, almost without thinking what he had said.

Sam stopped him before he could say more. "That wasn't his fault! He was drugged. I hope to god you didn't tell Sage that… did you?!" Sam snapped aggressively, looking to see if she had heard what her husband had said. Apparently she had not.

"No. Of course I didn't. Give me some credit! That was between you guys. I only found out when I read the report that Kane gave. I give him credit for admitting to it though, drugged or not…" Dan didn't finish.

"He didn't have a whole lot of choice, Dan. Corey died in his arms with a couple of witnesses, with guns brandished; standing over him… albeit that there is only me left to tell the tale. Hunter wasn't there at the time. I do know that Reese is still in love with Kane. I had hoped she was over it, but the look on her face when Kane told her to leave spoke volumes. She looked like she wanted to kill him when he rejected her."

"Yeah, I noticed. I think we all did, especially Kane. She has to have been in love with him the whole time." Dan said the words softly. "What worries me is what is he going to do about it? He hates her. Maybe she thought when Kelly was out of the way, she would have a shot at him. But judging by the way he looked at her that's never going to happen! And as for the child… I don't know where that's going." Dan paused, thinking out loud. "She did look a lot like Star though…" His voice trailed off, realizing he was just stirring it all up a little bit more. "Coincidence, that's all."

Dan smiled. Maybe he did know Kane well. He didn't really believe that his father-in-law had done that. He turned to look at his wife. Her expression was blank. She had heard, and by the look on her face she was shocked.

Sage now knew what she had feared. Something she could not tell them. If he had done it once, he probably had done it twice. She turned towards her young siblings and ushered them towards the waiting car. She, too, needed to talk to her father. She had to know. Kelly had been her closest friend and she owed her that much whether it drove a wedge between her and her father or not. She and Kelly had shared so much in the last few years. Like her step-brother, she, too, was waiting to question her father, something she was dreading doing.

Chapter 8

Kane's thoughts were in turmoil as they sped through the streets at the usual Branson speed. Snow didn't slow them down and Hunter had learned to ride as fast as Kane if he didn't want to lose his boss. This time Hunter took the lead and set the pace.

Kane had seen the child in the church and he knew Star had sensed the likeness to herself as he had. Why in god's name had Reese brought her to the church? He intended to ask her that question within the next half hour.

They rode for all of the half hour through the streets and Kane followed Hunter as he suddenly veered off the road and into a hotel driveway. Hunter stopped the bike as fast as he had started it. Kane stopped behind him and glanced up at the lavish looking building. It was opulent to say the least, even sporting a doorman who stood in a large black woolen coat and fur hat to match.

"Sir," stated the burly gentleman, "would you like any help there parking the motorcycles?" Obviously he didn't want a couple of cycles, albeit they were Harley's, standing in front of his coveted front entrance.

"Won't be here long enough to park anything, mate. We'll just leave them here where your good self can keep an eye on them. Okay?" stated Kane with his usual Branson arrogance. He half turned to his daughter. "You good to climb off there, Star?"

"Yes. I can make it." Of course she could, she was his daughter. It was harder getting off the bike than getting on, but she made it in true Star fashion and stood there waiting for her father to dismount.

"You sure we should leave the Harleys right here, Kane? Someone might take a shine to them. Expensive pieces of merchandise like these." What Hunter was trying to do was get Kane to work with the doorman as, quite obviously, Kane didn't want to, and what Kane didn't want to do... he didn't.

"Here is just fine, Hunter. How long we gonna be in there anyway? I only have a couple of things to say to her and then we can get the hell out of here. Right?" asked Kane somewhat irritated.

"Not quite right, Kane. May take a little longer than that. Might be some papers to look at..." Hunter didn't get to finish.

"You never mentioned that. You just said she wanted to talk to me." His voice got louder. " What the fuck else is going on..." and Kane stopped mainly because Star was staring at him, and so was the doorman, plus a couple of elderly well-dressed gentleman who quite obviously didn't appreciate Kane cursing in public and outside their hotel entrance.

Kane still sat astride the Harley and Hunter sat alongside him on his. Both bikes gleamed, polished to the enth degree. Kane glanced at the doorman and he looked at Star. She almost looked embarrassed, and that's when he gave in.

"Okay, so get someone to move them to the side. But there better not be one dent on this machine when I come back to get it... nor on his," Kane's voice was just a little threatening as he pointed to a small nook in the driveway, while climbing off his motorcycle at the same time.

Both men noted that the doorman was getting just a little edgy and might be about to call security.

Kane winced just a fraction as he stood up straight, and then reaching into the back pocket of his tight jeans, pulled out his badge, something he didn't do too often.

"This pretty much allows me to park where I want," and Kane flashed his badge quite vehemently in the burly doorman's face.

"I am so sorry, Commander Branson. I didn't realize... I, er..." Mr. Doorman was flustered, becoming a crimson color, which was exactly the effect Kane was trying to create.

"No problem… come on," and Kane took hold of his daughter's hand. "Let's get this over with." Kane was dreading seeing Reese again this fast, but more than that; he did not want to face the truth of looking at the child with her.

He marched into the lobby of the hotel with Star firmly attached to his hand, leaving the doorman looking like an utter fool. "Which floor?" demanded Kane, totally ignoring the reception area that contained tiny lavish fountains centered in the middle of the marble floor. There were flowers everywhere and crystal chandeliers hanging mid-ceiling. Hunter noticed, and then again he had noticed that when he had found where Reese was staying.

Hunter didn't like Reese, not just because she was in love with Kane, but because he saw her as a threat to bringing his boss down. He hadn't liked her the first time he met her in Iraq when they had rescued both her and Kelly from Ryan Holden's grasp. Something wasn't right about her, like she was hiding a very dark secret, one that he thought even Kane didn't know about… yet. But he had the feeling that they might be finding out very soon.

By now Kane had reached the open elevator. "I repeat… which floor?" He was becoming very agitated, and was engaging all kinds of numbered buttons.

"Sorry, boss… tenth. Suite 1001," replied Hunter, brought to a swift reality from the Commander.

When Hunter had made contact again with Reese after the rescue in Iraq it had been on Kane's instructions. An assignment, if you like, to find out more about Reese and her husband and why they were even in Iraq. Ambassador Jenkins was supposed to be there. His wife, Reese, was not and it had bugged Kane since then. Kane knew the whole time that Reese was still in love with him, but he was trying hard to push the thought from his mind that, somehow, she was involved in Kelly's death. Kane had been lured to Iraq to end the reign of terrorist Ryan Holden. Reese was also held captive there, but none of that would have got Kane there. Only Kelly being held there would get Kane overseas. Reese knew that fact and somehow Kane had this deep feeling she had passed the info onto Ryan Holden, possibly using it as a bargaining tool to save herself some grief and brutality at

Holden's hands. Reese said she was raped by Holden, a fact that was never proved. Kelly had been both repeatedly raped and branded by him. Holden had waited to get Kane for years. That chance had been presented to him… on a plate, and Kane thought that somehow Reese was the server.

The red velvet-walled elevator stopped at floor ten seeming only to take a few seconds to get there. By now Kane was more than agitated. Star could sense it and so could Hunter.

Star wasn't quite sure why she was there except her daddy wanted her to be, like he had something to prove to her. She was nervous, but there was no way she was going to let anyone know that, especially her father. She glanced back at Hunter. For some reason she trusted him also, even though she didn't know why.

Hunter stepped in front of Kane and arrived at the suite door first. It wasn't what any of them expected. On the door it stated it was the 'Ambassador Suite'.

"Appropriate," muttered Kane, but said with sarcasm.

Hunter knocked a couple of times on the door and felt sure someone was looking at him through the peephole. He was right.

The door opened and a tall, official-looking man in a pinstriped suit opened it, and then stepped back out of the way. He recognized Hunter from the last meeting and knew immediately who Commander Branson was from Reese's description of him, even down to the long blonde hair.

"Mr. McLeod. Nice to meet you again, and you, sir, are Commander Branson," he added with a very strong American accent and put his hand out to shake the commander's hand.

Kane stretched his hand to reciprocate the gesture, a little unsure of whom this was.

"You have the advantage. And you are?" Then it clicked. He was Reese's attorney, pinstriped suit and all.

"Mr. Davis. I represent…" he didn't get to finish his statement.

"You are Reese's attorney. Is she gonna sue me or something?" Kane half laughed. It wasn't a joke. He was putting the pieces together in his mind. That's why she came to the church… to make her presence known and to make sure everyone saw the little girl. He felt

Star's hand go limp in his clutch and Kane looked down at her. There was an ashen stare on her face as she looked into the room. Behind the attorney someone else stood there in the shadows, someone that looked like her.

"Come in, Commander. Ms. Wade is expecting you and so is your daughter!"

Chapter 9

Kane thought he heard what Davis said, but he wasn't sure. If he had heard him right, he was about to punch him out where he stood. Kane didn't have another daughter, except Sage, and she sure wasn't standing there in the room.

"My what?! I don't think so!" and Kane pushed past Davis and into the room still with Star attached to him and followed very closely by Hunter, who now foresaw a lot of trouble brewing. This fact had certainly not been mentioned at the last meeting with Reese.

Kane stared at the other child. He knew she looked like him. She looked very much like Star with brown hair. He looked passed her to where Reese was sitting on the couch, not bothering to look around the very expensive room.

"What the fuck are you trying to pull?! She's not my daughter and you know it!" Kane's temper, like his riding ability, went from zero to sixty in the same amount of seconds. "You and I never even slept together, let alone had a kid. What on earth possessed you to tell anyone that load of crap? And why are you even here, Reese? No one wants you here. You are the cause of Kelly's death." Kane reached the cream leather couch and leered down at Reese who didn't even look upset by his antics.

Slowly and deliberately she stood up. She was shorter than Kane but not by as much as Kelly had been. She smoothed her well-cut black dress over her shapely body, letting her long brown hair fall back over her shoulders. "No, Kane? She's not?" She questioned him. " Then I suggest you look at the DNA results that Mr. Davis has." She smiled, a false smile pretending not to be bothered by Kane's temper.

"Kane," and she turned towards the young girl with the brown hair, "meet Leila. Leila, meet your father!"

Kane didn't know whether to laugh in her face, punch the attorney or what. He only knew there was no way he was this child's father. Proving it was another thing. There was only one person in the world that could prove it and she was in the ground. No one else had been with him while Reese was with them. No one. Not even his daughter was with them when Kane had pretended to kill Reese for the American drug kingpin Miles Stratton.

Star pulled her hand from his grasp, not because she didn't believe him, just that she suddenly felt threatened by the whole situation. She was number-one in her father's eyes, even though Sam was the oldest and Sage next, Star was the favored child. Kane turned his head to look at her, and saw a sadness in her eyes that wasn't there five minutes ago.

"Star, it's not true! She is not my child," and he turned to Hunter. "Did you know about this?" Kane was mean and aggressive.

"No, sir. I thought we had just come to sign some documents about Iraq and then tell *Ms. Wade* to get the hell out of here. I am as confused as you." Hunter paused. "Well, almost…"

"If I may interject, commander, I do have documents that prove you are the father. The child has your DNA." Davis stated with great authority and began to pull pages from his dossier, flipping through them with great speed.

"And where the fuck did you get my DNA from?" Kane exploded and grabbed the papers from the attorney's hands sending them everywhere.

Reese laughed. "From the hospital while you were recovering from your wounds. Money can buy a lot of things, especially favors of nurses who are underpaid. But then you know what money can buy, don't you? You are a very wealthy man. Does a commander get that much money a year?"

That's when Kane lost it. Hunter looked at the expression on Kane's face and rushed to him, almost throwing himself in front of his boss to stop Kane from hitting the woman. Kane lunged at Reese and it was only Hunter grabbing Kane that stopped him from landing a blow.

"Commander… don't! If she calls the station, you will be arrested by your own force. Kane, think about it! That's what she wants you to do, and in front of a witness," and he blocked the way from Kane hitting Reese, much as he thought she deserved it.

"Get out of my way, Hunter …" Kane pushed Hunter, but his bodyguard didn't budge an inch. "I will kill…" and he stopped short of saying it.

"What was that, commander? You will kill her? Is that what you said, sir? I don't think I would be making threats like that right now!" Mr. Davis paused. "Why don't we all calm down and discuss this like civilized human beings instead of yelling at each other."

Hunter thought that was the most stupid statement anyone in the room had made so far. Kane… calm down? He didn't think that was going to happen any time soon.

"Boss… let's just get out of here. Get your lawyer on this. Let them sort it out. You're too upset to handle this right now and she is playing on that fact. She picked today on purpose. Think about it!" Hunter wasn't even sure Kane could hear him through the obvious anger and distress he was feeling right now. Reese had played the hand well.

Kane did hear him and he knew Hunter was right, and also as he had pushed on Hunter he felt his own heart miss a beat. He couldn't afford another heart attack that fast and especially not here. He straightened up and breathed deeply.

"Give me a copy of that paperwork… now, Mr. Davis, and let's get the hell out of here." His eyes fixed on Reese. "I don't know what game you are playing, or what you intend to get from this for yourself and the child over there, but I promise you one thing. That child is not mine and I will never submit to that claim. You and your fancy attorney had better keep out of my way. Better still… leave the country. You may be an Ambassador's wife, but this is still Australia and I am still the commander of the AFP and I have more pull than either of you."

"Actually, sir, Ms. Wade is simply *Ms. Wade*. Her husband filed for divorce right after Iraq. Seems he can't compete with you…" and Davis stopped speaking, realizing he was compounding the problems. He picked up the papers from the floor and handed a copy to Kane.

"Is that true, *Ms. Wade*? Is your husband divorcing you because of me, after I rescued you for him?" Kane's look was vicious and he was having a hard time both absorbing this and still trying not to hit her.

"It's true. Another week and I will be plain Reese Wade again. He couldn't stand the thought of you and me together and with a child..."

"Ms. Wade, I suggest you stop that right now. Commander Branson is a very strong man, and I am having a hard time stopping him here, and in a few moments I might have to let go of him. I don't think you would want that, as I certainly would not testify against him if he did hit you." Hunter even surprised himself at his self-control. He glanced at Star who had stood by the door the whole time just staring at the other child. Her face was totally blank. She wasn't scared and she wasn't angry. She was totally her father's daughter. "Sir? If you are ready, we should go. There is nothing more we can do here at this moment. Leila is obviously not your child and you make it more than obvious how you feel about Reese. So, we should go. Star, you ready?" and Hunter let Kane go, turning him very slightly towards the doorway.

"Ready," answered Star in a very grownup voice, still staring at the other child like she could wish her into the floor with her look.

Kane came to his senses. He was causing a scene and he realized the suite door was still open. And they could be heard, not a very bright thing to let happen. He pulled away from Hunter and walked towards the door, taking hold of Star's hand again as he went. He paused briefly by the other child. She looked distraught and was about to cry. Kane didn't want that. It wasn't her fault, but now was not the time to say anything to her. Now was not the time for anything except getting out of there. He had the papers, he had his daughter and now it was time to go. He didn't say one more word as he went out of the door.

"Commander Branson's lawyer will be in touch with you, Mr. Davis, and Ms. Wade I suggest you do stay out of his way while you are here," and with that Hunter, too, left the room.

No one spoke in the elevator. Hunter could not imagine what was going through Kane's mind. He stood like a man frozen in time clutching the papers in his hand. When the elevator stopped, they walked out of the hotel. Hunter hoped to god that the Harleys were in once piece and that Mr. Doorman was not going to harass them anymore than he had.

Outside in the crisp night air, Kane could breathe again. What on earth was Star thinking and what was he going to tell them back at the house. At this point he had no clue, only that his life had fallen apart around him and he wasn't sure right now if he even wanted to go on.

Chapter 10

By the time the two silver Harleys arrived back at the Branson household, it was pitch dark. The driveway lamps were turned on and with the sound of high-powered engines and screeching brakes, the adults of the family rushed into the courtyard in front of the house. Sam was the first one to the door and opened it wide for everyone to see what was going on. Sam didn't expect to see what he did.

"Kane, for god's sake, calm down," yelled Hunter literally stopping his bike next to Kane's and dismounted as fast as he could.

Star jumped off the back of her father's Harley. She hadn't been frightened of the insane ride back; she'd just never seen a temper like the one her father sported now. He was furious beyond all sanity levels, and she moved away from him towards the front door of the house.

Kane parked the bike, swung his leg to the ground, and promptly turned on Hunter. "You knew didn't you before we went there? Right, you knew!"

"I give you my word, I did not know," Hunter yelled back. "I told you I thought it was just for paperwork! Kane, for god's sake, stop it!" Hunter looked at the door from where the entire family had spilled out onto the drive.

"Oh, it was paperwork alright! I was served with a fucking paternity suit! How could you not have checked? How could you let me walk into that fucking mess?! Today… of all days. God damn it, Hunter. You are supposed to be my bodyguard in or out of the AFP… don't I pay you enough…" and he stopped dead realizing they had an audience and he had just said out loud what he didn't want anyone else to know.

Kane turned to face the family. Somehow, in those few seconds, it seemed hell had frozen over. Kane stared at Sam. He had not wanted his son to know before he could tell him. He wanted it to be on his terms. And Sage… she hadn't deserved this. She had lost her best friend today and now had this to deal with. Hadn't she always been on his side? Would she still be? He doubted that. He didn't care so much about Dan. Buchanan, well… Kane had a feeling he might have already known and kept the fact to himself. Hunter had been his bodyguard in Iraq, and before that, Japan. The privilege had continued after Kane's return to Australia, and not just for police work. Kane had paid Hunter from his own wallet to make sure he had someone on hand day and night, whenever there was trouble. And now there was big trouble with a capitol T.

"What?! What are you all staring at? Never seen a grown man angry before?" As he spoke his jacket once more came open and his white shirt pulled apart. The bandages and staples could clearly be seen in the lights from the house; so could paperwork sticking out from the inside of his jacket.

Sam saw it and spoke first. "Kane, let's go inside and discuss this. You don't want… well; you don't want a repeat of earlier today. It's way too cold and if it doesn't bother you think of Star." He looked to Hunter to help him.

"Kane, sir, let's go inside. Sam is right. I can get you…" yet again Hunter didn't get to finish.

"You got me into enough tonight! I'll go inside, but only for Star's sake…" and Kane scowled at Sam for mentioning earlier, and then took off brushing past the whole family, as he charged towards the living room like an enraged bull. As he went, he pulled the papers from his jacket and thrust them at Sam. "You should understand this more than anyone… here…" and Kane was gone.

"The little girl from the church with the long brown hair…" asked Sage, dreading the answer.

"She's *our* sister," stated Star in a very low voice and she, too, moved into the room behind her father, brushing the evening's snow from her shoulders.

"Dear god! You can't be serious? Did Reese Wade say it?" asked Sage, knowing if she said it it would be a lie.

"Reese did… and her attorney has the DNA results. She brought him with her to Australia. Unfortunately, it looks like it is true," added Hunter looking down at the floor, not wanting to believe it and certainly not wanting to make the facts worse than they already seemed to be.

"Dear god… not again! Wasn't the mistake he made with your mother enough? We have another sister? How many more brothers and sisters are there we don't know about?" asked Kane's eldest daughter, looking accusingly at Sam.

"Sage! I don't believe you said that…" chimed in her husband. "Stop… right there. You had no right to say that to Sam! God almighty! It's not his fault. Your father doesn't know when to quit, not Sam! No, I mean… shit!" and Dan stared at his wife like he had never known the real Sage till that minute, nor indeed, himself. Sage had held a grudge against Sam for something her father had done forty years ago and a couple of years before even her own mother had come into her father's life. And Dan also held it against Kane.

"While you two sort things out, I'm going after him. See what the hell is really going on." And Sam stormed away from her feeling perhaps he didn't know them as well as he thought he did, and possibly neither did Kane.

Sam found Kane in the living room clutching the flag from Kelly's coffin. Star was near him, the one sibling that still trusted and believed in him. The flag was the first thing Kane had seen when entering the room. Sam had laid it on the back of Kelly's favorite old couch, waiting for Kane to come home.

"Kane…" and Sam was about to rip into him, but something stopped him.

Kane turned to face his eldest son. His older face was one of utter sadness, and if Sam had not known better he could have sworn there were tears in Kane's eyes. "It's not true, Sam. I didn't sleep with Reese Wade. I own up to the women I have had sex with…" He didn't know why he was saying this out loud, especially in front of a ten-year-old child. But it needed to be said and his children needed to hear it. "Your mother was different, Sam. I…. well, you know. And Corey… I didn't know till after the drug wore off. It wasn't intentional. You know that. And I never cheated on Sage Jay, not ever… and **never** on Kelly. I would have given my life for Kelly…" It was too much to bear even for a licensed killer like Kane.

Tears streamed down Star's face and she flung herself at her father. Together they cried on each other and for a second became one… just as they had that day when Kane had set out to rescue Kelly in Iraq. The grief was Kane and Star's to share. He clutched her to him holding her like she might break and he would lose her forever. His link to Kelly and a life and woman he loved… and Star, the favored one, never wanting to lose her father, but feeling that right now she might.

Sam felt like an intruder. A part of Kane's life he could never share. There seemed to be a lot of those lately. But for some reason Sam still respected his father and he knew that what Kane said was true.

The eldest Branson son took a step backwards and turned through the oak door taking him back into the hallway, where the others stood. He whispered softly so that only he heard, "I believe you, Dad. I do."

Chapter 11

Sam met Buchanan in the hall. "Is he okay, Sam?" asked Buchanan tentatively.

"He will be, I hope…" and Sam turned to Hunter. "Are you his bodyguard… still? Is he paying you aside from the AFP?" Sam was begging to know the truth, his eyes questioning the other man.

Hunter could sense the animosity from Sam even though Sam was trying to hide it. "I… yeah, I am. He didn't want anyone to know, not even you, Sam. I followed him here today right to the church. Kept out of sight till the last moments when you saw me." Hunter looked at Buchanan, who today looked old and tired, like the last few years had caught up with him. "As Mr. Buchanan knows, I was with Kane even before Iraq. No one else knew."

"Even in Japan… ?" asked Sam.

"Yeah, even there. He wanted you to be there… but he felt that was asking too much. You have a life in Hong Kong. I guess, in a way, he was protecting you." Hunter paused and his eyes looked straight at Sam. "When he found out there was a 'you', apparently he could not quite come to terms with it. He felt betrayed by your mother and his friend, Giles Harris. He figured all AFP men were like him… loyal. But as you know they are not." Hunter leaned on the doorpost to the dining room. He felt now he had started he should continue. He could say this in front of Buchanan, as the ex-commander already knew most of it.

"When his friend Alex died protecting Kelly in your uncle's jail, Kane wanted to kill everyone in his path. But that meant you, too, and you were his son. Sam... he worships you, really he does, but he couldn't ask you to give up the life you had made to be with him twenty-four seven. Me? There is only me. No family, no ties. Just the job." Hunter cleared his throat and continued. "I know, Sam, what you think of me because I... well..." he hesitated, "well, because of my sexual preference, but I would never betray your father and I respect him completely. Funny," and Hunter smiled, remembering back, "I asked him once in Iraq did that make me less of a soldier now that he knew..." Hunter stood there. A big burley guy, long dark hair... hard to believe. He was a macho man like Kane. Another licensed killer... but one who would risk everything for his boss.

Suddenly, Sam felt like a jerk. Hunter had been there for Kane when he had not, and Sam had been against him for the wrong reasons.

Words made it to Sam's mouth. "I bet he said no, right?" and Sam stuck his hand out to Hunter, "and it makes no difference to me either, my friend." He didn't struggle with the words. He meant them. Hunter was possibly a better man than he was and had certainly earned the right to have his father's trust.

Hunter reciprocated the handshake with a solid, firm grasp.

"You knew?" and Sam turned his head to Buchanan, at the same time letting go of Hunter's handshake.

"I knew all of it. You had to see it in your own time, Sam. One of you is his son and one his bodyguard, and I have a feeling that he is going to need both of you now. And changing the subject, did you ask him if it's true about the child, Sam?" Buchanan had to ask at some point.

"He said it's not, and I believe him. Kane seems never to have denied any of his affairs and I don't think he is going to start now. I left him with Star. They both need each other. She is just ten. She is a child... well, in age anyway. She is probably more grown up than any of us, and he certainly needs her as much as she needs him." Sam leaned on the wall and opened the papers that the American attorney had given Kane. Right across the top was his father's name. Sure enough it was a paternity suit. "God damn! Does she want him that badly to do this?" Sam paused, looking around and observing the obvious. "By the way, where did Dan and Sage go?"

"Wondered when you would notice. They went upstairs after you took off after Kane. Seems they were not too happy with your father. Unlike you, they don't believe him," replied Hunter, glancing up the stairs where there was no sign of the husband and wife.

"Sage… of all people? She was there with him when he went after Stratton. Wasn't she there the whole time?" asked Sam of Buchanan.

"Apparently not. Kane and Kelly stayed at Miles Stratton's house at Malibu while Reese was visiting him there…" replied Buchanan.

"Oh, god, and Sage thinks what?" asked Sam, really thrown a curve that Sage, of all people, would not believe Kane. This he could not understand.

"Don't know, son, but I think we better sit down with your father and find out what really did happen, and then get him a good lawyer before he does something crazy."

Sam thought that was a good idea. Star and Kane had had long enough to compose themselves now. Sam walked back down the hallway ahead of Hunter and Buchanan to the living room and looked inside the door.

Kane was sitting on the couch and Star was curled up next to him, half asleep. She had cried herself into a kind of slumber and Kane had his arm round her shoulders. Kane looked up and motioned to Sam to stay quiet. Sam stopped and whispered to the other two men to stop also. Kane stood up and slid his arms around his daughter, half picking her up from the couch. She was only semi awake and the day's events had taken a huge toll on her. As he helped her out of the living room, she snuggled into his hair, just the child she ought to be at ten.

"Be right back," he whispered and with that Kane was gone along the hallway and up the stairs.

"I suggest we take a seat and wait for dad to come back." Sam glanced at his watch. He had meant to call his home in Hong Kong way back to let his girlfriend know he was safe and what was happening. He would ask her to close up the apartment and get herself and their baby tickets to Australia within the next few days. Her parents could check in on the place they rented and make sure it was safe, and then he would have his family out there with him all under one roof, literally all of them. He was thinking he should go and use Kane's phone and was looking around to see if there was one in the room.

"Over there by the window. One there. A telephone, right?" asked Hunter rather proud that he was that observant today.

"Right. Thanks." Sam ran his hand through his blonde hair. He glanced up at the ornate mirror hanging above the phone. Even he still found it strange to see an Asiatic guy with blonde hair, even though it was himself. He dialed the number for Hong Kong and his home. No one answered, so he left a message for the number there at Kane's house, a house he would soon be calling home.

"So you will be staying on, Sam?" asked Hunter, kind of glad that he was.

"Yeah, for the time being. Think that's wise, don't you?" said Sam, as he walked back to one of the more opulent leather couches and sat down. On the table in front of him was a tray full of fruit and suddenly he realized how hungry and tired he was. He had only been in Australia since last night and jet lag was fast catching up. "God, I am tired. Just realized it… I need to go to the hotel. Left most of my clothes there." He went to stand up again.

"They unpacked?" asked Hunter and motioned Sam to sit down.

"No. Still in the case. I didn't have time to unpack anything."

"Hotel? Room number? I'll have someone go get everything for you. What about passport and money…" asked Hunter as he pulled his mobile out of his jacket.

"All here with me in my coat. But I didn't mention to Kane yet I was staying here. He might not want that. I should ask…"

"Ask me what? If you can sleep here? Your room is ready. Always is when you are here. This is your home…" Kane interjected. No one had noticed him slip back into the room. He closed the door behind him.

He had changed into sweats and nothing else. No shoes, just bare feet. His hair hung loose about his shoulders and dark circles lined his eyes. He, too, was very tired. "Anyone hungry? I haven't eaten all day and I assume you blokes haven't either. Hunter, see if you can find Nanny Silvero. She will make us some sandwiches and ask her for coffee. Meanwhile, there is fruit in front of Sam and I would prefer something a little stronger to drink."

Kane didn't stop at the couch and just carried on by, till he hit the drinks cabinet. There sat several bottles of scotch and glasses just begging to be used. He took the top off one bottle and poured himself a rather large double. He could almost taste it before it reached his lips and when it did, it was gone in one gulp. He poured himself another and took it to the old couch. Sitting down, he faced his son and Buchanan, who sat along side him.

"And now, gentlemen, when Hunter comes back, I am sure there are things you want to ask me," and he downed the next drink just as fast, got up and poured himself another one.

He sat back down on the couch, and this time he brought the bottle with him. Seemed like the old Kane was back, until he leaned forward, and the silver K he wore round his neck dropped out of the sweatshirt top, and as it did, Kelly's K could clearly be seen hanging tightly underneath it.

Chapter 12

Hunter came back into the room, closed the door behind him and immediately saw the bottle on the coffee table. "Found the scotch then, Kane?"

"Yeah. You have a problem with that?" Kane asked sarcastically, not really giving a damn, and drank that one down as well.

"Not a one. Your choice to go to bed drunk, *sir,*" and Hunter sat down on a hard-backed chair to the side of Kane. Hunter changed the subject. "Sandwiches and coffee coming up. Hope you all like ham and cheese."

"Anything would be fine right now," said Sam, munching on a delicious green apple he had picked up from the plate on the table. He scanned his father's face at the same time. He knew Kane could drink with the best of them.

Kane shot Hunter a sideward glance and then started to talk. "As you know, Hunter and I went to see Reese Wade..." Kane stopped, due to the door opening, and Dan and Sage coming into the room carrying trays of food. "Nice of you to join us," Kane quipped nonchalantly, and moved his bottle of scotch to the floor beside the couch. He wasn't normally sarcastic to his own family, but he felt they deserved it today. He was disappointed that Sage, in particular, did not believe him. He didn't care as much about Dan, but his own daughter?

Neither Dan nor Sage said a word, and, after placing the scrumptious looking food on the table, sat down on the last of the remaining leather couches. Sage glared at her father. Here he was mourning Kelly and putting down a bottle of scotch. Why didn't Hunter stop him?

That's why he was there, she thought. Kane picked up a sandwich and devoured it in three bites. The others followed suit and ate them down like refuges that hadn't been fed for weeks. Both the ham and the cheese tasted good and they were decked with crunchy tomatoes and crisp lettuce. Not exactly macho food, but great tasting at this hour of the day. Piping hot coffee sat next to them, and all but Kane took a cup. He poured another scotch, instead, knowing full well it was pissing his daughter off, and that's why he did it. That amount of alcohol would never make him drunk.

"As I was saying, I talked to Reese Wade and she slapped a paternity suit on me claiming that her child is mine. Leila is the child's name and she is roughly the same age as Star. Firstly, it's the only time I have heard about this child in ten years and secondly, and the more importantly, I never had sex with Reese. So it would be kind of difficult for the child to be mine. As Sage knows, as she was there, I was with Kelly and told Reese I was not interested in her. And before anyone says that I didn't remember having sex with Corey till later," and he flashed a look at Sage, who looked straight at him, "yeah, I know you know, Sage, and if you didn't, you do now!" and he watched her drop her stare. "I would have remembered Reese!"

No one said anything. No one had to. The way Kane said it spoke volumes. Obviously, he had found Reese attractive at the time and had chosen Kelly over her. "She had an attorney with her, a Mr. Davis. They have my DNA… supposedly… obtained through illegal ways at the hospital. Seems money talks, even in hospitals, which you may want to look into, Hunter. Have some of the guys do it and see exactly who is a little wealthier in the last few weeks." Kane looked at Sam. "So you went through the paperwork yet or not? It's your strength, isn't it? Dig deep, son. See what you can find on that document that's false because whatever Reese says, that child is not mine!" Kane stood up and moved to the window. It was pitch dark in the sky and he stared out into the garden where the lights illuminated the driveway and the flowerbeds to each side. He could see the rope swing hanging from the giant tree that had been there since he was a boy. He'd played on that so much when he was young and now it sat lifeless, covered in a layer of snow. Even the flower beds were topped with white, fluffy snow, and he looked hard at the world outside, where everything seemed snowbound and equal. It was as if his life flashed by him, childhood to adulthood all in one go. And now he had another problem in his life, the day he buried his wife, a wife he could almost see sitting on the swing with Star on her lap. He whispered low. "Kelly," and he realized the whole room was watching him.

Kane felt the eyes on him. He turned to them all. In his mind he had come to a decision. "I have a feeling that this is something I am going to have fight… this with Reese. She couldn't even let me bury Kelly in peace, so I am sure she is not going to let this go. I know the truth and I hope, at least, some of you here believe me, and some of you will work with me. I think," and he paused, gathering this thoughts together, "that I should temporarily resign as commander. Let my deputy take over for a few months, just till things are sorted out. Deputy-Commander Stevens has been doing a good job while I was in hospital, anyway, so let him continue for another few weeks." He stopped again. "I need to get a lawyer and take Reese into court. I need…" Kane was slowly cracking under the strain. Suddenly he looked his age. He looked stressed and tired beyond belief. His chest hurt and the bandages pulled tight. Maybe they were keeping him together so he didn't break into tiny little pieces. Maybe.

It was his son that broke the tension. "I think that's a wise decision, dad. If it's okay with you, I will move in here, bring Sita and baby Mia here and stay as long as it takes, maybe longer. I am your friend as well as your son. We have worked together before and make a damn good team, right?" Sam stood up and moved to the window alongside his father, putting his arm on Kane's shoulder.

"Right, son. We do, and I would welcome you and your family with me here for as long as you want to stay." Kane didn't cry twice in one day, but he came awfully close to it. He had reserved the tears for his daughter.

"I'll send someone for your things, Sam, and help get your girl and child over here. We can arrange customs for you. They have passports, right?" Hunter stood up and once more pulled his mobile from his pocket and began dialing numbers.

"Yes, Hunter, Sita does and the baby is on hers. I left the number here at the house so hopefully she will call me soon." He half glanced at the phone hoping it might ring.

Even in Kane's state of mind he could detect a change between Sam and Hunter, like a truce had been reached, and he was glad. He needed them both on his side.

"Good job it's a big house, mate. All these grandkids and kids running around. Never be able to sort them all out of who belongs to whom," laughed Kane. He was trying hard to cover the way he was feeling and hoping to god he was.

As if on cue the landline rang. Sam looked to Kane, and Kane nodded for him to pick up the phone. It was Sita and immediately Sam got into a long conversation with her about bringing the baby and flying out to Australia.

Kane sat back down on the couch and left them to it. Hunter was busy on his mobile arranging things for Sam. Sage and Dan still had not shared their thoughts.

"So, Sage, your feelings on this would be?" Kane pitched right in. "I did screw…" and he tamed the wording down. "I did have sex with Corey, albeit I was drugged, but that's it. Not after I met your mother, nor after Kelly, was there anyone else, not one time." Kane wondered what was going through Sage's mind. She was like her mother, yet she wasn't. Sage Jay had ended up being a party girl and that's how she had died, picked up in a cab and driven to the airport, raped and murdered. And Kane had taken care of all the men that did it, one by one till they were all dead. A one-man army out for revenge… a bit like now. "Sage?"

She stammered through her words, her voice rising as she spoke. "I am trying hard to believe you, dad. Remember, I saw how much Reese wanted you and how much she helped with Kelly. She wasn't doing it for Kelly, but for you. She risked her own life for you. Anything she did was for you." She hesitated.

"Whose side are you on here, Sage? Hers or mine? What… you think I paid her back in kind? Is that it?" It was his turn to raise his voice. "You know me better than that!"

"Do I? You had sex with Kelly the day you met her to get what you wanted! You didn't know where that was leading… you didn't care! All you thought of was getting the job done. Taking down Walker and Miles Stratton, and you succeeded like you always do… getting the job done! That's always been your motto, dad. You let me go while you drank and my mother took to partying without you. Oh, I knew! That's mainly why I left home. No, dad, and then there was no mother to count on. It was too tough not knowing when you were coming home. I didn't blame my mother. I blamed you. You drank, dad. Like you are doing again now." Her voice got louder, so much so that both Hunter and Sam dropped their calls and her sentences came out in a garble of words. "You use women, you always have… and I have a feeling deep down that you used Reese Wade!" And now it was said… out in the open so that everyone knew her thoughts.

As Kane stood up, he picked the bottle of scotch up from the floor and hurled it violently at the fireplace on the opposite side of the room. It shattered into a zillion pieces, and the family photos on the mantel above rocked on the shelf. "You know damn well that's not true, young lady. How dare you speak to me like that! How dare you! If you were a man, I would kill you for that!" Kane stared at her, turned from them all and left the room, slamming the door behind him.

Chapter 13

"**D**ear god, Sage… how could you do that? If I had known you were going to hit him with that, I would have stopped you! I have known Kane almost as long as you have. That's not the truth," yelled her husband, "and you know it! Why did you do that?" Dan was yelling at the top of his voice at her. He hadn't believed Kane, but he certainly wasn't going to accuse him of that, especially not in front of his son and his bodyguard, two forty-year-old men that were as tough as nails. She had to be out of her tiny mind! Maybe he should go after Kane and then again, maybe he shouldn't. Dan had heard the last sentence loud and clear.

Sage was shaking from head to foot. She had meant it, but she had not meant for it to come out like that. Even she knew what she had said could not be easily undone. She was punishing Kane for the years he wasn't there to look out for her or her mother. Something that had seethed in her mind for all those years and now it had finally surfaced. Yet, without her father, she would still have been a prisoner in the compound where Kane had found her, or, by now, dead from dope. A compound run by Kelly's father, Walker, and one where he also found Kelly.

Sage slumped down on the couch, put her head in her hands and cried bitterly. She knew what she had done and her husband was right. She probably had lost her father's confidence for ever. "I'm sorry," she murmured through wracking sobs.

Sam spoke first. "I don't think sorry is going to cover it, Sage! He was truly hurt by what you said. I will go after *our* father and make sure he doesn't do anything stupid. And if he does, it would be no thanks to you!" Sam went through the doorway at the same speed Kane had and he, too, slammed the door behind him.

"I suggest, Sage that you stay out of Kane's way for the next few days. Let him calm down. He has enough to deal with right now without family turning on him. Sam and I will find him a lawyer if he doesn't have one and get this situation with Reese sorted out. Something has to be finalized or your father will snap. He may be a killer, but even those kind of men have a breaking point and I think Kane is near to it. You want to be responsible for that?" Hunter leaned down near to her face, as he spoke, trying to convey to her just what she had done. He turned to her husband. "Dan, get her to your rooms and, like I say, I would stay there for a few days, or at least out of his sight."

Dan nodded his head in agreement. He felt sorry for Sage, but he felt a lot worse for Kane, and, helping her from the couch, ushered her out of the room.

Hunter sat down on the now vacant couch and tried to collect his thoughts. One thing bothered him. Why hadn't the child been mentioned in Iraq? Admittedly there had not been much time to do so, but even so… something he would mention to Kane at a later date. His thoughts were disturbed by a loud banging of doors and men yelling. Hunter dashed out of the room and ran up the stairs to the bedrooms. The noise was coming from Kane's suite.

"Dad, you can't go out again tonight. It's bitterly cold and snowing again. Kane, think what you are doing! I know you are upset… I would be, too…" Sam was trying to make his father see reason.

"I am not upset! I am furious… Get out of my fucking way, NOW! And before you say anything else, I am not drunk. Half a bottle of scotch does not make me drunk!" Kane stood by the mirror on the back of the bathroom door. He pulled the sweatshirt top up and over his head. His whole upper torso seemed to be covered in bandages. "Enough of this crap, too!" He started to unravel them from his chest, dropping bandages to the floor as he went. The scar came into view, a good foot long and still raw. Most men would have died… but Kane was not most men.

"Dear god, Kane. I didn't realize it was that bad. I mean, we only saw you in the dirt… I… er… shit!" Sam was making it worse, and as he heard footsteps by the door, he turned to look.

Hunter didn't stop to knock and came straight in. "Guys, you can be heard halfway round the house." Even he hadn't seen the scar before and he stopped dead in his tracks.

"What!? What are you both staring at?" Kane hadn't looked before and he turned to view his body in the mirror. It was a mess. Maybe he had taken the bandages off too soon. Too late now and something both he and the family would have to get used to. A warrior's scars from battle.

"Okay. So I won't go out tonight… but tomorrow is a different story. You are either with me or not." His temper switched down a notch or two, and he picked up a robe from the white whicker chair, glancing round the room as he did. Everything reminded him of Kelly. Even though it had been weeks since she was in the house, Kane swore he could still smell her perfume lingering in the room. He moved across the bedroom to where the two men stood. It wasn't so much a bedroom as much as a way of life. Two large couches were strategically placed in the middle of the room and a huge TV screen on the wall visible from both. Book cases adorned the walls and on the far wall stood Kane and Kelly's bed. Now it was just Kane's.

Both men watched as Kane passed by the bed. It was obviously of Kelly's choosing. Kane more than likely would not have picked the pastel colors it sported and certainly not the velvet canopy overhead. Definitely a woman's touch.

Kane stopped at the couch. "I'm sorry, Sam. I have to come to terms with all this in my own way and Sage certainly did not help the matter tonight. Daughter or not, I don't know how to forgive her for what she said. On Kelly's grave, I did not sleep with Reese Wade," and he sat down on the small couch. "One of you guys get the scotch from by the Jacuzzi? It was Kelly's favorite place to have drinks and make love…" He smiled, a sad smile, and his faced was lined with memories.

"Sure. I'll get it," and Hunter proceeded to get not one, but two bottles from the small drink's cabinet in the bathroom. He picked up three glasses also. Maybe tonight they would all take a drink even though the clock was ticking away. He still marveled at the Branson inner sanctum of a marble Jacuzzi with gold-handled taps.

Hunter placed the bottles and glasses on the table in front of Kane and the now seated Sam, and poured them all a large glass each. Kane raised his glass just one time.

"To Kelly," he said and drank the scotch in one go. He didn't say anything else. He didn't have to.

"Kane," and Hunter breathed a heavy sigh. "Tomorrow we should get a lawyer for you. Have them go over the papers from Reese's attorney. Something, obviously, isn't right." Hunter paused. "I was thinking downstairs, why didn't Reese tell you about the child before, especially in Iraq? I know there wasn't much time to tell you anything, but you said that she stayed in touch with you the whole time after you '*killed*' her. This whole mess doesn't make sense. It would have given her a bigger hold on you. A way to keep you."

A puzzled look crossed Kane's face. "Yeah, it would if it had been true. But it wasn't, was it? It's like the child just appeared out of nowhere. And she could hardly say something that wasn't true in front of Kelly. Kelly was the only one that could say without a doubt that I was nowhere near Reese. She was with me at all times, even in the US. But you are right, Hunter. The child did just appear from nowhere. And why did her husband wait to divorce her now? Some story about he couldn't compete with me. That's a crock of shit! I've seen pictures of the Ambassador. He is a giant of a man!"

"I don't think that's what she meant, Kane… She's not in love with her husband!"

"Yeah, I know…" Kane leaned back on the couch and ran his hands through his long hair. "First thing in the morning call the AFP lawyer. Get him over here. See what he says about the paperwork and ask him to find out how she got my DNA." Kane pulled the sleeves up on his robe. He was full of pin holes from the needles used in the surgery. "Well, my arms aren't going to help us to much, are they?"

They were interrupted by Hunter's mobile phone ringing. "Yeah, right, okay. You're outside now? Just ring the doorbell and the housekeeper will let you in. Put the bags in the hallway, and Kane's son will come down and collect them." He paused. "And, Dave, I owe you."

Hunter hung up the line. "Your bags will be in the hallway in about five minute's time."

Sam stood up. "Thanks mate. Didn't like the hotel much anyway."

Kane waited till his son left the room. "Nice move, Hunter, getting Sam on your side. Nice thing to do by getting his bags for him. Help with customs, too, if you would. I need him…"

"I know you do, sir. I didn't just do it for you; I did it because Sam stopped judging me. And, yes, you do need him. The rest of your family is divided, and I think, sir, this time, you are going to need all the help you can get."

Chapter 14

When both men had left the room, Sam to get his belongs, and Hunter to show him his room and help him settle in, Kane moved over to the window. He sat down on the rocking chair that Kelly had nursed the kids on. He felt comfortable there and pulled one of the blankets that always lay there over him, leaned his head back and dozed. His dreams were fitful and a couple of times he awakened. He watched the dawn break over his land. It had always been Branson's country. Shades of pink filled the early morning sky and snow lay like a blanket on life, protecting it, keeping it safe, and he thought of Kelly beneath it. He reached down for the bottle of scotch he had set on the floor beside the rocking chair. There was a tiny drop left, not much, but enough to quench his thirst. For right now, comfort did come in a bottle.

There was a knock on his door. He didn't answer. They went away. He didn't want company right now. What he did want was Kelly… and another scotch. He couldn't have one, so he opted for the other. One wasn't enough, but the bottle was empty. Leaving the chair, Kane sauntered into the bathroom. There he found another bottle. In fact, he found two. One for a rainy day which he thought there might be many? He looked down at the bath. How easy it would be to climb in there and end it all… but that wasn't the answer, not yet at least. First he had something to do.

He took the bottle back into the bedroom, opened it and poured another. On the table was a tray of candies and a couple of apples. Feeling just a tad hungry, Kane downed them all, and another scotch. He looked at his watch. Six a.m. He could hear sounds in the house like folks were stirring; maybe he should think about joining them. Think about the lawyer he should talk to today and how Reese should be dealt with. Why on earth had she done this? His mind wandered.

Last night, when he changed into sweats, he had laid his gun on the table and it still lay there. Might not be a bad idea to keep it with him today. He always felt a little naked without it. Might not be a bad idea to get a shower, also. Discarding the robe and sweats, he went to the bathroom and took the hottest shower he could stand on his body. It hurt... badly. Soap was definitely a no, but at least the water made him feel fresher. One thing he could not hide too well was his breath and the alcohol on it. That wasn't too smart.

Pulling black jeans and a gray sweater from the closet, he dressed quickly and stuck his ever-faithful gun down the back of his expensive jeans, and pulled the sweater over the top of it. He tided up the room just a little. Isn't that why he paid a housekeeper?

Someone knocked at the door again. This time Kane answered. "Yeah, who is it?"

"Sam. Brought you some breakfast. Thought you might like some company," whispered Sam, not wanting to wake the whole household.

Last thing Kane wanted... breakfast. But he appreciated the thought. "Come in, son." Kane glanced round the room. "Damn!" He had left the brand new bottle of scotch on the table. He figured Sam would notice... how could he miss it?

Kane opened the door for Sam.

"Was hoping you might be hungry." Sam sat the tray down on the table and the bottle greeted him. He didn't say much. If his father wanted to drink, that was his affair. He wasn't about to stop him, not now anyway. If he kept on doing it... maybe. "Eggs, bacon, toast and orange juice. Goes down well with scotch." Sam laughed. It was the tension breaker that what was needed.

"Point taken. You eaten, Sam? Seems like a lot of food here." Kane had to admit that the aroma coming from the food made him extra hungry. Candies and apples had not quiet done it.

"No. There is enough here for both of us." Method to the madness. If Sam ate, Kane would not refuse to.

Kane knew that was the idea, but it worked anyway. They sat down on either side of the table. The eggs and toast went down well and Kane realized just how hungry he was. He finished off the plateful of food and drank two cups of coffee. Sam noticed.

"Hunter heard from the lawyer." Sam stated as he heaped more food onto his plate.

"At this hour?" Kane sat back in his seat still eyeing the food.

"He left a message for him and the lawyer called back sometime in the night. He will be over about ten." Sam now poured coffee. If his father wasn't hungry, he sure was.

"Does he know why he is coming?" asked Kane leaning forward and helping himself to more scrambled eggs.

"Some of it... not all. Thought you would want to explain to him." Sam paused mainly to sip his piping hot coffee. What you said last night about resigning... you still considering that?"

"For a time, yeah... until this is sorted out. The kids needs a parent, one who is here, not some father running round the world fighting crime. They only have me now." That made Kane think.

"No they don't, Dad. They have Sage. Okay, so she was way out of line last night, but she is still your daughter and we are all family and we stick together. There is me, Sage, Star, Kene and Kip and anymore kids you might have fathered along the way..." Sam waited for a reaction.

Kane looked at Sam and saw the twinkle in his eye. Kane's face creased first from anger then to a smile. Sam's eyes gleamed and Kane leaned across the table and shook his son's hand with a very firm grasp. His son... his ally... his friend.

They finished breakfast together. "Still snowing?"

"No, last time I looked out it had stopped, more or less. Just some flurries." Kane stood up and moved to the window to find out for sure. "Yep, just flurries." He glanced at his watch. Now nearly eight a.m. "What time did you say the lawyer was arriving?"

"About ten. Do you want to go over things with me?" asked Sam very tentatively.

"Such as?" Kane questioned, turning to look at his son.

"I don't know. Just thought you might want to go over stuff about Reese. Dad, you know I believe you. How did you think Reese fixed the DNA?"

"I don't know." He thought for a moment. "Son… do you know much about DNA? Can it be hereditary? I mean does it have to come from the mother and father?"

"Not quite with you? It can be planted, if that's what you mean" He looked at Kane. "That's not what you mean, is it?"

"No." Kane sat down on the couch once more, opposite his son. "After I came back to Australia and before I met Sage Jay, I was… well… not the greatest example of moral standards. I was young and free, I thought, and I dated a lot… no, I didn't date, I screwed around a lot…" Kane stopped, maybe telling his own son this made him sound like a complete jerk, with no morals whatsoever.

"Go on, dad. It really is not a shock anymore," and Sam laughed. "I've seen the way women look at you… I can't say I could blame you, and you didn't know about me back then… and?" Sam leaned on his hands which rested on his knees. He wasn't surprised and he couldn't say anything. He, himself, didn't have the highest standard either, till he met the mother of his child, and then that changed, just like Kane had when he met Kelly.

"And way back then I fell in with some guys and girls from the USA…" added Kane, pouring himself a scotch for courage.

"Really! Anyone in particular? Someone you were with a while?" asked Sam hopefully, pretending he didn't even notice the scotch.

"I can't remember. I used to drink a lot back then… okay, so I drink a lot now, too. But I moved around a lot, as well. All areas of Australia, Italy, America, England… you name it, I was there. Then the AFP offer came along and I jumped at the chance, especially with all the *credentials* I had. And then I met Sage's mom and I settled down. The rest is history."

"Italy?"

"Yeah… raced cars with Alexandria Vincentia. I taught him how to drive Formula one style. And then England, where I met Peter Graham. We all kinda grew up together, the three of us and then the girlfriends that became wives. You looked shocked, Sam. Yeah,

Kelly wasn't joking when she told you I won the British Grand Prix. I did. And Peter Graham was the Inspector at MI5." Kane paused and took a long breath. Seemed like a lifetime away now... a life that included Kelly.

"How on earth did you accomplish all of that in one life? You have lived ten men's lives! You really won the Grand Prix? I thought Kelly was just saying that because of the way you drive! My god, Kane! Huh, so my father won a grand prix!" Sam was overjoyed at the fact.

Kane watched his son. He was really proud of him. Kane smiled to himself. Sam might not be so enamored if he knew that he then drove his best friend, Vincentia, into a crash that killed him. He changed the subject.

"So that's why I was asking about DNA. I remember back at a recent training for the AFP that someone mentioned that it could be traced from grandparents to child."

Sam realized what Kane was saying. "So you think it might be one of your past affairs? But if it was, how would Reese fix that?" How would she find the right woman when Kane couldn't even remember them all?

"Good question. I have no clue. Maybe we should go talk to her again and take our lawyer with us."

Chapter 15

At ten o'clock, Kane, Hunter and Sam were seated in the library surrounded by baskets of condolence flowers from the funeral. Dan brought the lawyer into meet the family, or, rather, his father-in-law.

Kane was very composed for someone who had just buried his wife and been hit with a paternity suit all in one day… and had also downed a bottle of scotch before ten a.m.

All round the wall were bookshelves overflowing with volumes on the history of guns, and right at the end, by the door, on the lower levels were several rows of children's books. On the opposite side of the room to the couches were gun cases… all in Kane's collection… A very priceless collection of antique guns.

Kane stood.

"Commander Branson," the dapper lawyer stretched out his hand in greeting.

"Mr. Lewis. I am very glad you could come on such short notice. I hear you are one of the best that the AFP has," Kane stated, reciprocating the gesture back to Lewis.

Mr. Lewis smiled a wry little grin, knowing his reputation preceded him. Tall and thin, with short black hair and a moustache to match; Frank Lewis was about fifty, and sported a face lined with many years of courtroom experience.

Sam stood up also, and shook hands with the lawyer, and Hunter acknowledged Frank Lewis with a nod. Dan stood by the window. To him, the room seemed cold this morning.

"Commander, Hunter said you have paperwork…" Lewis had met Hunter before.

"Yes…" and he handed the suit to Lewis, "and the name is Kane."

Lewis nodded at Kane, sat down on a high-backed chair, and started to peruse the paperwork. He looked very serious. Kane didn't think that was a good sign. He sat between his son and Hunter, and hoped to god that Lewis didn't notice he'd been drinking. And for that purpose had munched a bunch of peppermint candies on his way down the stairs. Drinking wouldn't help his cause too much.

"Commander… Kane… this document seems to be in order. Somehow, Ms. Wade obtained your DNA. The child's DNA and yours match. No doubt of that. What isn't here, though, is her DNA, Ms. Wade's. That's a little strange. One would think it would be here, especially as she claims to be the mother. What this does prove, without question, is that you are a relative of Leila." Lewis looked straight at Kane.

"What? Now I am confused. So she is my *something*? A relative? What else could she be? And in front of my family, I once again state… I did not sleep with Reese Wade. I will take a lie detector test to prove it." Kane already looked a little agitated. How could she be a relative?

"I think your word is good enough, sir, for now, anyway. What we need is to get Ms. Wade's DNA, and see if it matches the child's. That's where you might be able to find out what is really happening." Lewis paused. "Is there any chance that she is related to you that you can't remember?" He coughed. "You ever had any… er … affairs… that may have led to this child…" Frank Lewis stopped speaking, mainly because you could cut the air with a knife. He glanced round the room. It was full of weapons, mostly guns. Not a very comforting thought.

"You mean did I sleep with anyone in the last ten years other than my wife… !" and Kane stopped because he had. Corey.

"That's not my business, commander. What is my business is if you had one about eleven years ago with someone who could have produced the child with your DNA."

"Stop right there, Mr. Lewis! I did not have any affairs after I met Kelly, my second wife. And my youngest daughter, Star, is older than

Leila. Does that answer your question?" Kane was obviously quite upset by this line of questioning.

"Adequately! I am sorry if I upset you, but if this goes to court, they will ask you questions like this and much worse." Lewis was blunt.

"Then it must not go to court, Mr. Lewis. The Commander is very well respected as you know, and this would not be a good thing for the AFP." Hunter had been sitting quietly up to that point. "Can you get Ms. Wade to have a test? I mean, legally? And without any problems? It really needs to be dealt with quite quickly, don't you think? If she insists it's her child, I would think she would be glad to take one, even just to keep a hold on Kane." Hunter had a brain and he was using it.

"I agree with you, Hunter. I think this entire matter should be dealt with using the utmost speed and secrecy. The courts would be a very bad way to go, especially for the AFP, and for your boss." Lewis had figured by Kane's response that he had something to hide about his past and judging by the way he got so agitated would not do so well in court. He put it down to the fact he had just buried his wife, and the alcohol he had obviously consumed today. "We should take a trip to her hotel and confront her. I think, myself, you and the commander should be there and possibly Sam. You have a telephone number for the hotel, Hunter, and we will call her right now." He pulled out his mobile.

Hunter gave him the number, without even looking at his boss, who by now either figured he was interfering or was glad he had taken some of the heat off him. Obviously, he should not have been seen to be agitated, and Kane thought that Lewis probably realized he had been drinking. What an utter mess. If only he had done the thinking with his brain...

But something at the back of his mind was nagging at him and he couldn't figure out what. Something from his past, way back after Nam. Some girl or girls... he couldn't quite remember. He would have to start trying, though, and fast. He did know one thing, how was he going to keep his temper under control in front of Reese.

"What if I step down for a while? I was talking about it last night. Take some time off with the kids. They only have me for a parent..." 'Oh, great line', thought Kane. 'A parent like me!'

"Not a good idea, commander. Makes you look guilty," commented Lewis, his face creasing in a frown. He dialed the number and moved across the room, while he carried out a conversation to the hotel.

"Guilty of what?!" Kane wasn't so quiet this time, and stood up turning towards Lewis.

"Dad… let it go. He's right," Sam stood also and faced Kane. "Let him set up the meeting. He can do the talking and you just keep quiet… for once in your life!" Sam was even shocked at himself speaking to his father like that. "He can tell you have been drinking, and he knows what's going on in your life. Let Lewis do what you will be paying him for, ok?" He stared straight into Kane's eyes. A mirror reflection looked back. There was a kind of understanding between them that no more words were needed.

Kane nodded to his son and turned away and moved to where Dan was.

"He has to stop drinking now before it gets a hold of him. I know he can take a lot, but now is not a good time to be doing this. You going to tell him or am I?" Kane's demise was Hunter's concern.

"You do it. He won't listen to me about alcohol. He might listen to you because of the AFP. You are the one that stopped him doing drugs. Speaking of which, he had to be in some pain still. Are they giving him anything for that? That scar was pretty mean-looking, even for a tough man like my father. Did they give him anything for the pain?"

"Yeah, they did. Morphine for the first few days, and then he refused to use it." He glanced at Kane. "One stubborn father you have there, Sam. Sometimes he is the hardest man to work with."

Sam thought that was a strange statement from Hunter like they were still hiding things as they did back in Iraq. He wondered if Kane had disclosed to Hunter that there was something in his background about a woman. Maybe now was the time to find out. Kane was talking to Dan, and Lewis was still on the phone.

"Hunter, did dad ever mention to you about some American girls he met after Nam? Just wondered if he had." Sam waited with some hesitation for the reply.

"Very briefly, probably about the same time he told you, I guess. Sam, I have to know what is going on in his head. It's my job. After Japan there were people looking for Kane, not just Ryan Holden and his merry band of terrorists. The AFP could not have their top agent, who happened to be their commander, running round without back-up. I was picked to go with him wherever he travelled. It's hard not to become close to someone on that basis. He had told me so much, especially about the past with Kelly and when he met you for the first time. You are very lucky, Sam. He is a great guy and if he has to hate someone for stopping his drinking then let it be me, not you. Like you, I believe him about Reese. I knew she was here and so did he. What he didn't know was the paternity suit and neither did I. What I did know was that she was about to make another play for him, I just didn't know how she would do it and, to be honest, Kane had every right to be angry last night outside in the driveway. It's my job to know and I failed him! But whatever it takes, it will not happen again!"

Chapter 16

Nanny Silvero, long time live-in housekeeper for the Branson's, ushered the children downstairs to see their father before he left for the hotel.

Star stood back while Kip and Kene talked with their father. He knelt down on the hardwood floor, more to their size, and tried to explain where he was going. They were way too young to know why.

Sam watched Kane. He was so different with the children. They didn't see the killer in him. They only knew the father figure. He also saw Star watching Kane. There was a kind of look in her eyes like Kelly used to have, almost like some kind of written understanding between them.

When Kane said goodbye to Star she clung to him, and he whispered in her ear. She nodded her head very slightly and closed her eyes.

This time they didn't take the Harleys, but the limo, which mainly sat in the garage unused. Hunter drove them through the snow and even with that hindrance only took them a half hour from the house to the hotel. The whole way there Frank Lewis briefed Kane on what to say and what not to say when they met Reese.

Pulling into the driveway of the hotel at twelve-thirty, they had a few minutes to spare before the meeting. Kane wanted a cigarette. As the limo pulled up, Kane opened the door himself and stepped out, not waiting for Hunter. He disappeared to the smoking area with Lewis following after him, still trying to school him in what to say.

Hunter let the valet take the car and he and Sam waited in the hotel lobby.

"Wonder what that's about? Your father doesn't like being told what to do. I hope Lewis doesn't push it too far with him. I don't think he wants to be on the end of one of Kane's tempers!"

"I don't think so either... none of us do!" Sam paused. "Not sure how he is going to handle Reese. You said he didn't do too well last night in the hotel."

"No, he didn't. But to be honest, I could not blame him. We thought we came to get paperwork on Iraq and he was handed a paternity suit instead. Not your usual evening out, but not your usual day, either. I am sure he will be fine," Hunter stated, hoping that that would be the truth, but he somehow thought it might not be. His boss was already agitated and that wasn't good, and now, Lewis was just letting the situation escalate. He was keeping an eye on Kane just in case his temper flared.

Kane pulled his cigarettes out of his leather jacket and then the lighter from the back of his pants. He lit up one cigarette, finished that and lit up another. He blew smoke rings into the cold air, mainly to show a somewhat rebellious attitude towards the lawyer. When he finished the second one, he decided that was enough nicotine. What he wanted was another scotch... at almost one p.m. Even he knew that was wrong. He half-listened to Lewis and looked up to see where the other two guys were.

"Think we should join my son. We don't want to be late for *Ms. Wade*, do we?" Kane was sarcastic as he spoke, and started to walk towards the hotel noticing, yet again, how resplendent it was. How on earth could she afford this? Her husband, yes... but not her.

"You ready, dad? Even I hope we are not here that long. Didn't care for her the last time we met..."

Hunter led the way, back across the marble floor, to the elevator and then to the tenth floor. He knocked on the suite door. The attorney opened it and spoke first, peering at the small party on the landing.

"Right on time, Commander Branson," acknowledging Kane first. "Come in. I see you have a full team with you. Thought you might, so, we have security with us, just in case!"

Kane started to speak, but Frank Lewis stepped in first, both into the room and with his voice.

"Well, that's good. Obviously, you don't trust us and we don't trust you. Very smart of you," and Lewis moved to Reese Wade. "And you must be the lady of the hour, Ms. Wade. I have heard a lot about you in the last few hours, some good, and some bad. Now, I get to see for myself." Lewis didn't banter words, just went straight in there.

The attorney didn't look too pleased after hearing that statement, and closed the suite door behind their guests.

"I assume, Mr...." Davis questioned like he didn't know.

"Lewis, Frank Lewis," retorted the dapper little man.

"That you have read the papers. As you would have seen they are all in order." The American attorney stood there with a very arrogant smile on his face, confident he had the upper hand. Reese was seated and never offered to say anything while barely glancing at Kane. Leila was not present, seemingly that she wasn't going to be present either.

Both Sam and Hunter stayed by the suite door. Neither said a word and neither was introduced.

"Everything seems in order, Mr. Davis... Commander Branson appears to be the father... or maybe a relative... but there is no certificate for the mother. How do you explain that? No DNA test results." Lewis pulled the papers from his attaché case and flipped through them.

"And why would my client need those? She is the child's mother!" Davis came straight back at Lewis, almost leering at him.

"Is she?" Lewis paused for effect. "We only have yours and *her* word for that fact. I would like Ms. Wade to take a DNA test and we should arrange that as soon as possible, like today or at the latest tomorrow. And while we are on the subject where is the young lady in question," asked Lewis looking round the suite. "I don't see her and would like to hear what she has to say. If she is ten she should be able to give us some information. And, maybe, she should take another test in front of a neutral witness, you know... all by the same lab, even the commander here should take one... again!"

Kane went to speak.

"Dad, don't say anything. Let Lewis say it for you. He can say it better than you can and he is tying the guy up right now," whispered Sam to his father.

Kane half-looked at his son and simply nodded in reply.

"So, Mr. Davis, can we meet Leila? Is she here, maybe in the bedroom?" And Lewis moved towards the bedroom door. Security stepped in his way in the shape of a big burly six-foot guy who looked like he had escaped from a Rambo film. Davis looked him up and down more for effect than anything else. "I guess we can't," and feeling he had made the point moved back across the room to his own group sporting quite a smug smile on his face.

"What time tomorrow is good for you then, Ms. Wade?" The question was direct.

"I don't think that is necessary. The child is my child. Ask Commander Branson? Right, Kane?" Reese was going straight to the source. She still knew exactly how to get to him.

Wrong button for her to push and Lewis knew it. "My client is not at liberty to discuss that with you anymore, so please, Ms Wade, drop the act. You may have muscle from the hotel, but we have the truth on our side." Now, Lewis was bluffing. "If this needs to go to court, so be it. The Commander has a very high reputation in the force and in this part of the world, and I would think, madam, that after he saved your life, you would be somewhat grateful to him and not want to drag his name through the mud." Lewis smiled... his voice on a completely even keel. Lewis had a feeling that he didn't want to look at Kane's face right now, and that he was more than likely ready to rip the woman to shreds, and he really could not blame him.

Lewis was right. Kane was seething and his temper was bubbling under the skin. If she made one more crack, he would not hold back. He hated her now. Once, maybe, a long time back, she would have had a shot at him, but not now, not ever. He couldn't take the stress of her. He watched her sitting there, legs crossed cold and calculating like she was paying him back for the rejection he had showed her.

"I really don't think I should be subject to the DNA test for my own child. I have birth records and details you might want, and I did not come here to argue about it. I came for Kane to do what's right by his daughter…" That's all she had to say.

Kane exploded. He glared at her and his comments were both rude and arrogant.

"Ms. Wade. Unless you had an immaculate conception and the child came out looking like me, there is no fucking way that that little girl you are hiding most carefully is mine! You, and I, both know that we never ever had sex, except in your dreams, and we will prove that…"

He was interrupted by Reese's maniacal laughing. "Really, Kane, then how do you explain Leila? She looks just like Star… and you. Even your own daughter noticed it in the church yesterday! Must have been pretty hard to see another offspring when you were burying your wife… I wonder how many more children you have that you don't know about…" She never finished the sentence.

Kane lunged forward knocking a small table out of the way as he went. If it had not been for the hotel security and Hunter holding him back he would have reached forward and killed Reese Wade.

"Don't think this is the end, Reese! If you were a man, I would kill you for that!" Kane was more than angry. He really did want to kill her. He pulled his arms from Hunter's grasp and turned to the now open door and marched out of the room with Hunter in tow. Composure was lost. Sam went after them, and Lewis grabbed the papers and left the room.

"Well done, Ms Wade. We now have the commander exactly where we want him. He threatened you in front of witnesses," Davis whispered to her. "You will soon be a very rich woman!"

Chapter 17

Kane didn't wait for anyone else. He took the elevator down to the ground floor and hurried outside. The pain in his chest was getting worse by the second. He reached in his jacket, pulled the pills out, and took one without hesitation. He must not let Lewis see him as a weak person. He knew he had to get out of the room after his outburst with Reese, and had felt the sharp twinge as Hunter tried to restrain him. When would Kane learn not to antagonize the situation of his heart? But Kane also knew he wanted to kill Reese. Never had he felt such hate towards one person, especially not a woman. She had hit him where it hurt the most.

Kane moved to the side of the hotel and leaned on the wall. He was shaking mostly from anger. He was also breathing hard and was angry at himself for losing it in front of witnesses. He smacked the wall with his bare hands, sending the snow splattering around him.

"God damn it! She knows how to push my buttons!" and he hit the wall again, this time attracting attention from Hunter, who was looking for him.

"Kane, you okay? That wasn't the smartest thing you…" Hunter started to speak.

"Don't you think I fucking know that? I should have just walked out when I had the chance." Kane stopped as he saw Sam and Lewis coming out of the hotel. "Keep them both away from me. Get Sam to distract Lewis long enough for me to calm down and get my breath…"

"A bad one?" Hunter screwed his face up at his boss.

"No, just need to calm down before I get in the limo. Wish the bike was here. I could take off on my own for a while… need a break…" and he meant that literally. For some reason Kane had the awful feeling that all the tests were going to come back on Reese's side. She was too confident and quite obviously she knew more than he did. His face was lined with worry and this was unusual for Kane.

Hunter watched his boss carefully and knew Kane was cracking. It didn't take a terrorist like Ryan Holden to do it, just a conniving woman such as Reese Wade. "Kane, maybe you should take a break… just for a few days. I'll go with you. Sam should wait for Sita, and then maybe join you and me, and bring all the kids with him. You and I take the Harleys and head up the coast. Maybe tomorrow… after the DNA tests are finished with. Apparently, Lewis arranged them already. They are at 3 p.m. today. They rushed them through because of your status."

"Really? I still have status?" Kane laughed a kind of crazy laugh and flashed his electric-blue eyes at his bodyguard.

"Of course you do," Hunter questioned. "So what do you say? Just for a few days, get away from the pressure. I know Lewis said not to resign, but he didn't say you couldn't take a few days off. Just throw some things in a bag and go!"

Kane looked at Hunter like he was totally nuts… and yet, maybe, he wasn't. Maybe clear his head and get away from Reese before he really did do something he would regret, and, also, would stop him chasing shadows in that bedroom at home.

Hunter expected a fight. He had his reasons ready to go back at his boss… toe to toe.

"Okay, you win! Tomorrow we go. First light. Get these DNA tests done today. They can call us with the results. Takes about three days anyway."

Hunter was taken by surprise. "Right, okay, great. Go up the Gold Coast." He was shocked it was so easy. Too easy. He had expected a fight and he didn't get one. What was Kane up to?

Kane was now composed back to his original status, and leaving Hunter standing there, took off for the parked limo. Climbing into the car, Kane leaned back in the seat, closed his eyes and gave a great impression that he did not want to be disturbed. This was his way of telling them to back off. Sam and Lewis also climbed in and sat down, as Hunter jumped in the front seat and turned the engine over. Lewis started to speak, but after a warning glance from Sam, decided against it.

An hour of travelling along the main roads of Sydney brought them to the hospital that Kane had become so familiar with in the last few weeks. This time Kane wasn't the first out of the car; Sam was, and he virtually had to persuade Kane to get out of the limo. There was a huge reluctance on Kane's part to go in the place. Lewis walked behind them.

"Nothing to worry about, Dad. We all know what the results will be," said Sam and walked with his father and Lewis into the lab, leaving Hunter to make calls. Sam slapped his father on the back, and together they walked through the doors of Kane's future.

"Do we, Sam? I have this nagging feeling Reese is holding the trump card. She was way too confident. Something she never was, even as a US Marshall." Kane paused, "I wish that I could remember more after Nam. The American girls…"

"Would be helpful if you could, but if you can't, then it's no crime…"

"What did you say?" and Kane stopped in his tracks, and stared at Sam.

"I didn't mean anything by it… I just meant it's not a crime…" Sam was looking at his father; in fact several people in the hospital lobby were, too.

"Crime… it was something to do with a crime and some girls on a holiday here from America." Kane was frantically trying to remember, but forty years back was a long time to remember every detail of life. It would come to him… it had to.

"You could check the files… you have that power."

"Yeah, I do, but it wasn't here. It was Alice Springs… I would need to go there… exert some power as Commander."

"What on earth were you doing there?" questioned Sam, while undoing his coat, then folding it across his arm.

"Been there many times… few years back with Kelly and the new recruits, before I came to Hong Kong…" Kane stopped. He couldn't talk about her today, and concentrated on Lewis. "Mr. Lewis… you are the lawyer here. You have any associates in Alice Springs?"

"One or two. Why? You think you know someone there that could help?" Lewis was more than happy to assist if he could. Earning an even bigger name for himself than he already had had plenty of appeal for him.

"Maybe…" Kane's brain kicked into gear again. "And before I forget, Hunter and I are taking a trip tomorrow at first light. Gold Coast. Thought it might be a good idea to get away for a couple of days. The tests are never back till after three days or so, and we will be back then. We both have our mobiles with us. Hunter will give you both numbers before we go."

"You're serious aren't you?" Lewis asked, knowing full well that the commander was.

Sam was about to question his father concerning the Gold Coast and realized he was telling Lewis that was the location.

"Yeah, mate, I am. So let's go do this and then we can get home. Got packing to do." Kane issued the statements so methodically and without flinching. He slipped his leather jacket off and made ready for the testing. "Ready, Mr. Lewis? I can see Mr. Davis and his merry band up ahead of us. And Mr. Lewis, I will control my temper with Ms. Wade, just keep her away from me… right away, you understand?" Kane's face said it all. If Lewis had any doubts how mean Kane Branson could be he didn't now.

"I understand very well, Commander Branson. That will not be a problem. Ms. Wade will go first then leave, and next it will be your turn. So you wait here and I will go to the door and make sure all is right with the tests. Sam, look after your father for a moment."

Sam nodded to Lewis. "You just told him the Gold Coast. Both you and I know you are not going to the Gold Coast! Why did you tell him that? Just so you and Hunter can go and cause havoc somewhere looking for something you think happened? And what do I do? Just sit home and wait for your call to rescue you again? Is that it?" Sam wasn't too happy.

"Yeah, something like that, son. Something just like that," and Kane winked at his son.

Chapter 18

In the crisp morning light, Kane and Hunter stood next to the Harleys. They had a couple of changes of clothes wrapped in bedrolls, some food and water, mobiles, AFP special credit cards and ID. Kane looked up to the house. Snow clung to the ivy. It still looked strange for Kane to see snow just outside Sydney. Once in a blue moon or rather century. As he looked up at the windows, he thought he could see his youngest daughter there in the lamplight; her hand pressed against the window just like it was when he left for Iraq. He closed his eyes and shook his head. She was still there. He waved at her, and the lonely figure waved back.

Kane thought back to yesterday. The DNA tests at the hospital and the ride home afterwards. The tests went fine… the ride home somewhat quiet. Reese had gone right in there and given her blood. She hadn't even flinched when they asked her for it. This had posed questions for them all, especially Kane. Lewis had been quiet in the car as well. On arriving home, Kane, Hunter and Sam had spent hours just talking and trying to sort things out. Sam was the only one who knew what they were doing and where the two men were going. Neither Dan nor Sage was included in the discussions. Kane had given Nanny Silvero instructions and then spent time with the children, especially Star, who seemed totally to understand what he was telling her. Star looked sad that he was not taking her with him. She went along with the idea that her dad would be back in a couple of days, and if he didn't come back, the children could fly to him. This idea was one that Kane had no intention of letting happen. Nor did he think they would be back in a couple of days. Alice Springs was almost a two day drive, maybe one and half the way he and Hunter rode Harleys.

Kane waved again at Star and blew her a kiss, turned to his bike, mounted it and kicked it into gear. Hunter did the same and the two men took off down the drive towards the gate at a low speed, hoping not to wake the rest of the house at five a.m. Only one other person watched them go and that was Sam. He had agreed to stay at home both to wait for Sita, who was due on the next flight from Hong Kong, and also to keep an eye on his siblings. Kane had implied that he didn't quite trust Dan and Sage now. A sad reflection in his mind left by Sage's accusations of the other evening. He wanted to trust her, but he couldn't. With that in mind he had a taken a very late night ride to the cemetery to visit his wife's grave. It was cold and dark, but Kane had found the fresh grave still covered in flowers, with just a gentle icing of snow on top. He had kneeled in the snow, touching the brand new headstone and fingering her name, not believing she was dead. He had whispered her name, and cried gentle Branson tears and then he was gone, into the darkness, like an apparition he was becoming.

They left the driveway of the Branson estate and they were gone into the shrouds of the half-light, zero to eighty even into the hazard of the snow. Made no difference. They powered down the main street without the distraction of traffic at this early hour. Both cops dressed in black leather, one with long blonde hair and one with dark. Neither wore helmets...ever. Two totally different men joined together, yet again, for a mission.

Hunter had mapped out the route for them and he led the way, having learned to ride this fast to keep up with Kane's general speed. Now, he enjoyed the ride. From Sydney to Adelaide, and then Port Augusta. Hunter figured they could do that before nightfall if they kept the pace they started at. He knew Kane could generally stay on the bike for at least a day without rest and urgency seemed the most important thing here. The only thing that worried him was Kane's physical stamina. Everyone seemed to forget that Kane had a scar spreading right across his chest and that in his jacket he kept pills for his heart. Kane was one tough bastard and he was the one who seemed to forget this the most.

By six a.m., the light was almost on their side. They knew that they had concrete roads for now and the Harleys would be most comfortable on those. Hunter had made sure that the two way radio on the bikes was working, just in case they needed them on route. As they got further west the snow was disappearing from under their wheels, which made travelling easier on the tires. Hunter picked up more speed and Kane followed suit. The quicker they got there the better and the more time they would have to find any information they needed. One hour turned into two, and then three, before Hunter thought maybe they needed a pit stop.

Hunter made a right off the highway and into a small town he had seen from the road. He flagged Kane down and they stopped in front of a petrol station. It was now just past nine a.m.

"Thought we might take a ten. Fill the bikes up and use the bathrooms. Looks like an okay kind of place. You wanna go first? We shouldn't leave the Harleys to fend for themselves. Someone might take a liking to them; and leave us without rides aside stealing a hefty amount of money from us." Hunter laughed. They were cops.

"Right, mate. We don't exactly look like cops, do we? Keep our credentials in our back pockets though, just in case, along with our guns in our jeans," and Kane disappeared into the men's room, did what he had to do and resurfaced as Hunter finished filling up his machine.

"Want me to fill yours up?" he asked of his boss.

"Yeah. You want any coffee or something to eat? I'm starving!" Kane was already disappearing into the little store and heading for the counter, not waiting for Hunter's reply.

Inside the early morning coffee-shop Kane ordered two strong coffees to go and two ham sandwiches on brown bread with all the trimmings, a couple of apples and some candy for later. Stuffing the candy in his jacket pocket and preparing to pick up the coffees, Kane didn't seem to have room for the sandwiches.

"Help out with the food there, sir?" asked the skinny young man that had made them. He wiped his hands on the apron he wore and picked up the food he had prepared with some haste.

"Yeah, thanks," and Kane paid for the food with cash, giving the young man a tip.

As Kane approached Hunter, he nodded to him and Hunter left the bikes and headed for the men's room.

"Thanks, son, for the help. Just put them on the seat. Bit warmer now. No snow anyway." And Kane unzipped the jacket. He turned to get something from the back of the bike, and the gun in the back of his jeans could be quite clearly seen.

"Wow, mate... powerful looking gun. You a cop or something?" and the young man did a double take, suddenly gaining a new respect for the man in front of him. The long hair had not fazed him, but the sight of the gun did

"Or something... yeah, something," replied the commander.

"Where you from?" asked the boy very innocently as he pushed his fingers like a comb through his floppy hair.

"Sydney..." Wasn't a very specific answer, just general.

And then Hunter was back, and picking up the sandwich, unwrapped it and devoured it like he hadn't eaten for two days.

"You a cop, too, mate?" asked the boy and had Hunter almost choking on the food.

He looked at Kane. Big piercing eye look, implying 'what the fuck'...

"Saw my gun..." whispered Kane.

Hunter nodded, and then continued with the sandwich.

"You on a job, sir," the young man asked, his eyes bobbing like apples in a barrel.

"You could say that... yeah, a job." It was the truth.

"Exciting... I envy you!" The young man heaved a sigh. "I am stuck here... nothing goes on here. One day... one day, I will leave here and go to Sydney. See what a big city is like and get a real job." His voice was wistful and how he wished. He kicked the gravel with his well-worn shoes.

"Well, son, if you do," and Kane fished in his jeans pocket and produced a card, "if you do, call this number," and he handed him the card for the AFP. "Someone there will help you."

"Thanks, Mister." The young man peered at the card. No name of a person on it, just a number of the main office of the AFP. A huge smile spread across the youth's face and he returned to his station at the counter, pushing the card into his pocket.

Kane hurriedly ate the sandwich. For some reason he wanted to get going again. Ten minutes had turned into twenty, and they were burning daylight. Both men mounted their machines and took off with the same roaring speed that they had come in with. All Kane had done was give the youth a chance, something he would come to bitterly regret.

Chapter 19

Another three hours of riding. It got just a little warmer as they went along. They were not making the time as good as they needed to. There was no chance of reaching Adelaide by nightfall and Kane was getting just a little bit agitated. He missed the alcohol and Hunter knew it. They needed to eat again and by now the time was just slipping by. Kane felt his mobile buzz a couple of times in his pocket, and thinking it was Hunter, just ignored it. He would check it later. If it was that important they would have kept trying. Around three, they pulled into a biker-bar alongside the highway. Kane did anyway. Realizing his boss was not behind him, Hunter turned back, slowing the speed to look for him. He should have guessed where he would want to be at this time of day.

Hunter parked the bike by Kane's next to a long line of Harleys and other assorted expensive bikes. This was one place the machines wouldn't get stolen from. The joint was a real biker bar, and even though the pair didn't look like cops, they were not dirty enough in dress to be bikers, and bikers were nosy enough to ask. Hunter could imagine Kane telling them the truth, that they were cops. Hunter pushed the squeaky door of the bar open to see Kane already chatting to a couple of guys as a few ladies seemed to be heading his way, too.

"Nothing changes for him," muttered Hunter. "Where Kane is, the women are… ."

"Hunter, over here…" yelled Kane, above the noise of an old jukebox playing Elvis Presley's 'Suspicious Mind' and the usual pool table chatter.

Hunter moved through the haze of cigarette smoke and people to get to Kane.

"Got you a beer, mate… ice cold…" and Kane handed Hunter the long glass that had been perched on the very well-frequented bar. It was a little warmer now. "Well, it was ice cold… mine was…" Kane took another swig of his, wiping the froth from his moustache.

Hunter took the beer and looked at Kane. Come to think of it, Kane did look like a Hell's Angel, with all that hair on his head and face, and no one would dispute the fact in there. He still wondered how he explained them being there. After all, it wasn't a bar that one would just drop into.

"So you a cop also, mate?" asked the 'tall Angel', the one with biker girls hanging off his arms, and a completely shaved head with an eagle tattoo on it.

"Sure, today, I am," and Hunter laughed. Second time today he had been asked that. So Kane had said that yet again. How did the man get away with it?

'Tall Angel' spoke again. "Kane, here, says you guys are riding up to Alice Springs for the week. You should ride with us, mate. Whole bunch of us going there. Meeting up with more blokes for a rally. Safety in numbers. What ya think, Kane? You wanna join us? Sure could use a gun like that with us…"

Kane had let them see he was carrying? Had he lost his mind? Then again, it would be a great cover to ride with a gang. They would go by totally unnoticed.

Kane glanced at Hunter, hoping that he didn't disagree with the new plan.

"Sounds good to me. You guys riding again tonight?" Kane was praying they were.

"Yeah, about a half hour. Wanna get closer to Adelaide and, then, Chico over there," and 'Tall Angel' pointed at a dark-haired angel, "has friends in a little town with a house where we can stay for the night. Plenty of booze and women… fix you right up, mates…"

'Oh, that will be a fun sight to see,' thought Kane and this time he didn't even look at Hunter. Good job he didn't. Hunter was glaring at Kane with great displeasure.

'Tall Angel' stuck his hand out to Hunter. "Boise. That's my name, after some place in the USA. My dad was from there," proclaimed the new friend.

Hunter reciprocated the gesture. "Hunter." Only thing that concerned him was that they had taken to the pair very quickly. What else had Kane said to warrant this?

As if reading Hunter's mind, Kane slapped him on the back. "Told them we are bounty hunters, after a chap who shot at some bikers…" And Kane didn't get to say more. He was approached by two 'lovely' young girls in the shortest of leather skirts it would be humanly possible to ride in and not be arrested. Their arms were covered in tattoos and their T shirts left nothing to the imagination. If they were twenty-one, that would have been a stretch. To bring that up now would have been suicide in a bar full of tough-looking bikers aged between eighteen to fifty… Correction to sixty, his boss, who could easily pass for fifty.

They almost but wrapped themselves round Kane and another one approached from Hunter's side and slid her arms round his back. He handled it well… considering. Kane almost choked trying not to laugh; instead he started a conversation with the girls, just bantering between the two very pretty 'hookers' that had latched onto Kane. Kane being Kane just took it in stride, being very used to women falling at his feet.

"Ladies, meet our new travelling companions. Watch out for his big gun though," and Boise laughed a crude and very dirty laugh. "Kane, they are yours!"

"Married, mate," Kane said it without thinking. Instinct. But it was a way out of having to spend time with the girls. Then again, it would be a good cover. "Separated, trying to put things right."

"Then, still yours! Drink up. You and your buddy like another?" asked Boise.

"Why not…" and two turned into three. Kane would rather it have been scotch, but at least it was alcohol. The scotch would come later.

Kane leaned on the bar like he owned it, with a girl on each arm. Hunter was trying to send him signals that he wanted to talk to him. Kane finally got the message.

"Excuse me, ladies. My buddy wants to chat. Be right back." He left them both propping up the bar.

Hunter ushered Kane outside. "Okay, Romeo…. What's the deal here? You must have some angle for travelling with these guys. You don't do anything without a reason."

"My mobile kept buzzing while we were riding. Need to check it and didn't get the chance yet. When I pulled up, Boise was outside with the bikes. He began admiring my Harley complete with the Australian flag on the gas tank. Said he had never seen one like that before. Asked where I was from and was I alone? He said the cops were just looking for lone bikers." Kane laughed. "Told him I was waiting for you to catch up. Surprised you didn't see the bar as you sped on by…" Kane quipped.

"I saw it. I was hoping you didn't. But you probably smelled the fumes from the highway. And then you told them you were carrying? Why would you do that?" Hunter was a little exasperated.

"Why not? Half the guys in the bar are. And this gun is not an AFP gun, so how would they know? It isn't the first time I have been mistaken for a biker…" and Kane remembered back to Mexico and hunting Stratton, which led him right back to Reese. He shivered.

"You okay, Kane?" asked a concerned Hunter.

"Yeah, fine. Just memories." His thoughts were catching up to him. "Then I found out that aside from the Aussie accent, his father was from the US and they are on their way to Alice Springs. Seemed like a great cover for us. So I tried to be friendly and blend in." He looked down at his clothes, "A little bit over dressed for bikers. But we have jeans, boots and leather jackets. We can just do away with the sweaters. We will fit right in. In fact…" and Kane took the jacket off and removed his sweater, stuffing it in with his clothes, and then slipped the jacket back on just zipping it at the bottom. The scar could clearly be seen adding an even more biker look to the dress code. "And if they look at my arms, I will certainly fit in!"

"And you want me to do the same?" asked Hunter.

"Yeah, why not…" as Kane spoke, his mobile buzzed again. This time he fished it out from the jeans pocket.

He flipped it open and saw it was Sam calling.

"Hi, son… was it you calling before? I haven't checked yet. We just stopped for… something to eat." Best not to say to drink with Hell's Angels. "Can you speak up, son? Hard to hear you" He paused, listening. "The kids ok? Who is missing? You are joking, right?" He was trying to take it in. "When? How long back? From this morning? Maybe she went home… no, I guess she didn't. Who noticed her gone? Really? And the child? She's still there? They will find her. She's probably out trying to wreck more lives… son, I gotta go. The line is breaking up. Must be where we are. Let me know when they find her, okay? Hunter and I will keep going, you know up the Gold Coast, unless you need us back there. Okay?" and Kane lost the call.

"What? What is going on… who is missing?" Hunter was putting his leather back on.

"What do you know? Reese is missing, since this morning!"

Chapter 20

Kane's expression didn't show sadness or happiness. Hunter stared at him. "She is what? Missing? How can she be? She has the child, her attorney and hotel security. You sure that's what Sam said?" looking disbelievingly at Kane.

"Yeah, I am sure. She probably went out on her own somewhere or is doing this on purpose. Wonder if our lawyer told her attorney we were taking a break? Didn't think of that… maybe I should try to get Sam back on the phone and see what else has happened." Kane started to dial the number back to the house. It would not connect. "Damn. Must be our location. I will try again as we get further along tonight on the trip."

Hunter had pulled his phone out, too, and was getting the same result. He stuffed it back in his jeans pocket. "So what next, boss… I mean Kane? You still gonna ride with the guys from the bar?"

"Even more so now, until we know what is happening back in Sydney." Kane leaned against his bike, resting against the leather seat.

"You okay, Kane? Has to be a shock for you. Maybe like you said she just took it on herself to leave," but somehow Hunter did not believe his own statement. Something somewhere had gone wrong and he had the distinct feeling that Kane thought the same. Kane had an alibi. Sam and he, himself, had been with Kane the whole time that they knew of, that was.

What Hunter didn't know was that Kane had left the house after everyone was asleep just to ride to Kelly's grave. He had pushed the bike down the drive so as not to wake anyone. Maybe, he should have woken someone. This thought was going through Kane's head right now.

"Yeah, maybe, but somehow I don't think so..." There was a worried look on Kane's face. He paused and took a deep breath. "Hunter... last night... after you all were asleep... I... well, I went out again. Took the Harley and went to Kelly's grave." Kane stopped and waited for the explosion from Hunter. It came.

"What the fuck did you do that for? On your own?! And now Reese is missing? How long have you been comm... ...." and he stopped abruptly. He moved in extremely close to Kane. "Did you? Did you go by her hotel? The truth Kane! Did you?" Hunter was furious, his face and dark features only emphasized by anger.

"No. I thought about it, but no! I didn't go anywhere near there. Why? You think what? That I had something to do with her disappearing? If I had, she would be six feet under!" Had he really said that out loud! Stupid move.

"That's just what worries me, Kane! Did you?" He grabbed Kane by the lapels on his jacket, almost pushing him and the bike over.

"Take your fucking hands off me, and don't ever put them there again, *mate*, or it's you that might be six feet under!"

Hunter immediately let go. Kane could fire him for putting his hands on a commanding officer, especially 'the' commanding officer, and Hunter also thought there might have been a double meaning in the statement. He backed off, and hoped that the commander was telling the truth and also that there was only one meaning to his statement.

Kane was glaring at Hunter, eyes of steel burning holes through his bodyguard. He felt betrayed that Hunter would even think that. But obviously he did. And if he did, then others would, and that was not good.

"Maybe you should go back! And I will go alone to Alice Springs. Might be better. Then you wouldn't have to keep tabs on me, would you?!" Kane wasn't calming down anytime soon. "Wouldn't want you to be implicated in anything, would we?" He pushed his phone into his jacket and pulled the cigarettes from the back pocket of his jeans and as he did, Hunter offered him a light.

Kane hesitated, and then accepted the light. The cigarette tasted good and he blew smoke out into the afternoon light. Now, he wanted a scotch. Hunter knew it, too. He turned to the back of his bike and opened his travel bag. He dug deep and then produced a hip flask full of scotch and handed it to Kane.

"You fucking son-of-a-bitch! How long has that been there? I wondered why I couldn't find it at the house!" and Kane grabbed it from Hunter's hand. He unscrewed the top and downed a couple or three gulps.

"Better?" asked Hunter, still standing his ground and still with the feeling Kane just might send him packing. He hoped not. It was obvious Kane needed someone, even just to yell at.

"Yeah. I should have told you I was going. I just wanted some time with her on my own…" Kane stopped, pausing to collect his thoughts. He screwed the top back on the flask and handed it back to Hunter. "You keep this with you for now. I'll ask you for it when I need it."

Hunter nodded and returned it to his belongings just as Boise emerged from the bar.

"Hey, mates. We need to get going. Want to get to Chico's place before sundown. You ridin' or you leavin' us?" Boise was followed by his Angels, all twenty off of them, laughing and very rowdy

"Riding. We'll be right behind you." Kane was emphatic.

"You okay to ride, Kane?" Hunter knew a lot of alcohol had now passed his lips.

"Fine, just fine." Kane turned to Boise just to let him know all was okay. "Just some business I had to deal with. Sorted now." And Kane swung his leg over the Harley and purposely let the gun show in the back of his jeans, and his jacket open slightly. His hair hung down over the back of his leather and more than one of the girls noticed him again.

"You want company on your ride?" asked a willowy blonde that looked all of sixteen. With painted face and nails, possibly pretty underneath the makeup, short leather skirt, striking five-inch high heels and a yellow T shirt that hid less than it ought to.

"Sure! You go zero to eighty, darling?" Kane asked her, turning his head to acknowledge her advances to him.

"I do more than that!" she smiled at him, painting her lips with her fingertips.

"I bet you do!" he retorted almost instinctively.

"Maybe you would like to find out later!" and she swung her leg onto the bike behind him, wrapped her arms round his waist and waited for the ride to begin.

"Maybe I would!" and Kane raised his eyebrows to Hunter.

Hunter climbed on his machine, pulled alongside Kane, and hoped to god one of the girls didn't want to ride with him.

The noise of twenty Harleys was thunderous. Each one revved the throttle, each bike raring to go. Kane felt the phone vibrate again. He knew it was bad news. Sam wouldn't call again that fast if it wasn't.

"Unless it's something else, your phone is vibrating against me," laughed the girl. "Your pocket is, anyway."

"I know. I'll get it later. By the way, you have a name?" asked Kane over his shoulder.

"Yeah. It's Kelly, Kel for short," she yelled to him over the noise of bikes and the smell of burning oil.

If it was possible for Kane to turn ashen, it was then. His heart missed a beat. What in God's name were the chances of that happening? Hunter heard it, too.

As the entire gang pulled out into the highway, Kane leaned back on the bike and felt the girl riding behind him. The memories flowed through his mind of Kelly riding with him. He felt the girl's arms round him, tightening as they picked up speed, riding two abreast, and Hunter next to him, they sped into the evening light.

Kane had a feeling that this night would be one he would not forget, and a gut instinct told him also that Sam's call spelled impending doom. He was right on both counts.

Chapter 21

"**A**ny luck reaching dad?" asked Sage, whose face was tear-stained from the day of crying. He had left without saying goodbye to her.

Dan had his arms round her, feeling that even she deserved his support right now.

"Left him another message, but he might not get it. For some reason neither his nor Hunter's mobiles are working right. I would rather have told him personally. Not sure how he is going to take it," stated Sam. Even Sam didn't know what to make of it.

Reese Wade was officially listed as missing. Buchanan had called Sam to update him and he, too, had tried to reach Kane without success. Hunter's mobile, also, was not reachable, so he stopped by the house to see just exactly where Branson was.

Sam was not so happy to see the ex-commander and hoped he didn't ask exactly where his father was headed to. He couldn't lie, but he certainly could not say that he and Hunter were on their way to Alice Springs. Maybe it wouldn't come up, and, maybe it would.

"So, when did you hear from Kane last?" asked Buchanan, removing his heavy coat and dropping it onto the back of the chair.

"About an hour back. But the signal was bad and we lost contact." That was the truth.

"Yeah, I tried, too. It's normally a pretty good connection up the Gold Coast. Wonder why it's so bad? Hopefully, Kane will touch base later," added the older man.

'I don't think that's gonna happen, especially when he gets the message I left him,' thought Sam, and turned away from Buchanan so his face would not betray his thoughts.

Sam sat down on the couch next to Sage and Dan. He kinda felt sorry for his step-sister, but she had brought the wrath of Kane down on herself. No one had made her speak to Kane like that. If for some reason he never came back, she would only have herself to blame. Perish that thought! He hoped Kane was able to listen to the message before he called back to the house.

Kane thought about the phone buzzing in his jacket, knowing the news was not good. But they had to keep going and this cover was perfection itself. He also felt the girl behind him and the closeness of her body. He wondered what she might expect from him later. Maybe he could drink so much that he would fall asleep. Then, he remembered that had never stopped him before. He had made love to Kelly so many times while drinking…

It was almost dusk as they turned from the highway. Both Kane and Hunter had moved up through the ranks of the Angels, seated comfortably one row back from Boise. Kane rode with ease, legs stretched on the bike, one he knew so well. Hunter still next to him, smiling. Kane was so at home being a Hell's Angel.

Boise had said they were going to a house. He didn't mention it was a ranch located just on the outskirts of Adelaide. As they pulled into the driveway a bunch of bikers, already gracing the lawns, converged on them, including men, women and children of all ages and nationalities. Trees surrounded the property, and included the house and some sheds that seemed to stand to the left of the main house. Kane could only imagine what was going on in there. Perhaps right now he should forget he was a cop and look the other way.

Parking the Harley, the willowy blonde climbed off the back, or rather slid off, but she didn't offer to leave Kane. He wondered if she was there to keep an eye on him, planted by Boise. The friendship had sprung up to easily between him and the top Angel. Kane also wondered if one of the guys in the gang had recognized him, after all he had been on several covers of The Police Gazette in recent years. The way to go now was slowly, just in case.

His companion was obviously not leaving him.

"Hunter… you have the scotch handy?" as Kane requested the hip-flask. He figured he couldn't be seen to turn down the advances of Kel, but he didn't want to take her up on it either. Not that she didn't attract him… because she did. Just bad timing. He took the flask and drank more down. "You like some?" he asked the girl handing it to her.

"Sure," 'Willowy' replied and she put her pretty painted lips on the flask and drank.

'Well, that didn't work,' thought Kane. 'Now what?' "You been here before?"

"No. That's why I am sticking with you, Kane."

"Really? Going to be interesting, huh?" It was then he remembered he hadn't told her his name. Maybe she had heard Boise say it… maybe not.

"That… and because I recognize you!" she said flippantly.

"Bikers all look alike, darling!" and he tried to brush it off, not even glancing at her.

"Maybe so… but they don't appear on the front of The Police Gazette too often though, *sir*!"

Kane looked staggered and failed to hide the fact. He leaned back on the bike and looked to Hunter, who looked just as bemused as Kane did.

"That why you rode with me? So you could keep tabs on me for Boise?"

"No… so they didn't find out who you are. Boise trusts me, so he didn't mind one bit when I asked him if I could ride with you. In fact, he thought it quite natural for me to go after the good looking new guy on the block."

"Thanks for the compliment, but just how do you know me… yeah, I know you said on the cover of some magazine, but you also knew my name!"

She leaned into him and he could smell the perfume again like he had on the bike. She whispered close to his face.

"Commander Branson, I would be derelict as an officer if I didn't know you, now wouldn't I?" and she flashed her eyes mischievously at him.

He didn't speak. He just stared at her a few seconds before words managed to escape from his lips. He pulled her to him and held her there. "How the fuck do you know that?"

"Problem over there, Kane?" yelled Boise, as he hugged one of the girls to him, his hands on her backside. "She gives you any trouble, you let me know, mate."

"No problem. Just getting to know her a little bit better," and Kane encircled her in his arms more to keep her there than to be nice. "Now, young lady. I think we need to talk, don't you? Hunter will mind the bikes…" and he marched her away a few feet making it look like they were really getting to know each other better.

He slid his arm round her waist and let his hand fall slightly below that onto her backside. She held onto him a little worried that she had showed disrespect to his rank. Even though she was from Alice Springs, she knew Branson's reputation… the professional one and the personal. Everyone did.

"Spill! If I was who you think I am, what on earth would I be doing riding with bikers? Think about it…" his eyes glaring at her, staring a hole through her.

"Good point, but I still know it's you, sir, and I am not about to blow your cover. There has to be a very good reason you are here and maybe the same reason that I am, and, oh, I might look sixteen but I am twenty six. They picked me because I look young and I guess tarty. But I assure you, I am very good at my job. The department…" Kel went to say more and before she could a man came out of the house and started yelling towards Kane and Kel.

Long dark hair and big… dirty, filthy clothes and carrying a knife. He was heading straight for the pair, yelling obscenities at them.

"Friend of yours?" Kane asked her sensing they were in for a visit.

"Never seen him before in my life…"

"Think he *knows* you…" and as Kane said that, the man proceeded to charge at them with a knife brandished in front of him.

Instinctively Kane pushed the girl behind him and out of the man's reach. He lunged at Kane.

"You fucking bastard… that's my girl!" screamed the man. "Get your hands off her, now!" The man leered at Kane. Yellow teeth bared at him and the stench of his piss-stained clothes filled Kane's nostrils.

"Calm down, mate... she just rode with me... I was just..." Kane was trying to explain and was wondering what the hell was happening.

"I can see what you were just going to do... you bastard!"

Kane jumped out of the way of the knife as the blade glistened at him. He now knew the guy really meant it... he was being set up. It was a test.

"If that's the way you want it..." and Kane pulled off his leather, wrapping it round his hand and arm for protection. He had a gun. What he didn't have... was a knife.

"Kane... !" and Boise threw him his knife, handle first.

Kane caught it. He turned and faced the guy full on. Hadn't he done this before... brandished a knife at someone to save Kelly?

The light was fading fast, but the lights from the property were enough for him to see his opponent. He had to fight him. He had to show face. There was no other way. Kane lunged at the guy hoping to knock him so hard he would fall back. Obviously, the guy was on drugs or had drunk so much he didn't know who was who. His blow hit the man and they both fell back together. Kane on top, but the guy caught Kane's s knife arm and held it above his head. He had to break free. Normally he could with ease, but the surgery from the knife wound was slowing him down. Hunter could see it, like in slow motion. Kane could not fail this test. With all his strength, Kane pulled the man to his knees. He didn't know how, he just did and with one thrust of the blade, slid it into the guys right arm. It was over in seconds.

Immediately, the guy dropped the blade and grabbed his arm in pain. Kane stood up, dripping sweat and still with the knife in his hand, a puzzled look on his face. He had been going for the heart and, at the last moment, had switched aim to the arm he had cut wide open. All the memories of Kelly and Ryan Holden came flooding back.

Kane flung the knife into the ground, yelling at the top of his lungs as he did. Kel clasped her hands to her mouth as she saw the scar across Kane's chest. Now she knew for sure it was the Commander.

Boise was the first to speak… "Your partner okay, mate?" and he looked at Hunter, eyes scrunched as he spoke.

"He'll be fine… last man that attacked him like that is dead! Kane cut his heart out!"

"I can totally believe that. Totally," and Boise moved to help the injured man, completely convinced that Kane was a killer and just what they needed.

Chapter 22

Kane walked back to the Harley. He removed the jacket from his arm and slid back into it, zipping it as he spoke. "What the fuck was that about?" He was openly angry, but also conscious of being watched. "Where's the girl?" and Kane turned back to make sure she was safe.

'Willowy' was right behind him. She was shaking from head to toe. Kane had performed rather too well. She knew he had a reputation but this went above and beyond that. "You alright, sir?" she asked tentatively.

"I'm fine and for god's sake stop calling me sir. You were the one who wasn't going to blow my cover, remember?! The name is Kane!" He turned to Hunter. "It was a test, right? They were watching?"

Hunter nodded at Kane, implying he was still being watched by about a dozen bikers. Hunter couldn't help notice the look in Kane's eyes. The look of a killer. "It was a test and I don't think it's over yet, but I do think you passed with more than flying colors. Boise was very impressed with you. But tell me?" and Hunter stood his ground well. "Who exactly were you trying to kill? The Angel or Ryan Holden? Holden, right?"

"Right," replied Kane and proceeded to pull his hair back in a band and tuck it into his leather. He inclined his head towards the girl. "So, now she knows more than she should. She needs to stay with us, night and day, no matter what. Understand?"

"Isn't Boise going to be a little bit suspicious if she only stays with you?"

"Us!" replied Kane flippantly, getting much more composed than he had been.

"Us?" echoed Hunter. His eyes wide.

"Yeah! Fake it!" came the reply from his boss.

"Thanks!" replied the bodyguard.

Kel ran her hand along the leather seat of the bike, giving Hunter a very quizzical look as she did. "I think you are stuck with me. I can at least explain what I am doing here. I thought it was the same as you, but I guess not. Oh, and I am not twenty-six or sixteen. I am twenty-one." She looked at the dark-haired man in front of her. "You his partner?" the word was emphasized just a little too much.

Kane could not hide a laugh.

"I am his bodyguard... not that that is any of your business." Hunter paused, thinking about her statement. "And he," inclining his head at Kane, "has five kids... no make it six at the last count."

Kane glared at Hunter. That wasn't funny.

"You're married then..." and she stopped, remembering the news in the Gazette about Agent Kelly Branson's funeral. "Kane... I'm sorry." She turned away from him wishing to god that her brain had not let her mouth run away with words.

"It's okay... really... I... ," and Kane turned away from the bikes into the fading light, pulling his cigarettes and lighter from his pants as he did. He lit one up as he walked and watched the smoke rings circulate up into the air, a night air that at least was not as cold as Sydney and no snow in sight. He wondered how his kids were doing today. "Oh, crap!"

He remembered the mobile and the message now on there. Only one missed call. He listened very carefully to the message. The words 'Dear God', escaped from his mouth. It was official. Reese was missing and Sam had told his father not to come back. Apparently, someone had seen him leave the house last night. Star had found herself to be hungry and went down to the kitchen to get some milk and a biscuit. She had seen her father leave and had told only Sam what she had seen. He hadn't said a word to anyone else, but he had to tell Kane, especially now. Soon they would be putting two and two together and coming up with the same thoughts Hunter had had.

Kane closed the mobile and stamped out the cigarette under his boot. He watched Hunter and 'Willowy'. Both kept looking his way, making him wonder just what they were talking about. He knew he was dragging the girl into a mess and he was going to have to tell her something. She might even be able to help in Alice Springs with records of past crimes there. Boise was a different matter. He was using Kane and now he knew that. But what 'Willowy' knew on the right side of the law, Boise might know on the not so right side. Problem was what was his price? If the drugs were being grown and harvested here and taken to Alice Springs, there would obviously be problems with the police. He guessed that's where he came in. Hired gun! What Boise didn't know was he was hiring a cop. What Kane knew was that if the police there recognized him, he was done. He would be arrested, commander or not, in connection with Reese's disappearance. He had said he would kill her in front of witnesses. And he still had to find out exactly whose child she was, which took him right back to where he was now. Puzzled.

He wandered back to the Harleys and his new friends. "Sorry about your man there, Boise, but I was just defending myself as you could see. Why on earth did he attack me like that? I was hardly touching her and surely that's common place around here!"

"Don't even worry about it, mate. He's crazy. He's been here for years now and every time he sees a new girl with a good looking guy, he thinks it's his old girl friend. Thanks for not killing the old bastard. I thought you were going to! Some day someone will," and he shook Kane's hand. "How's she working out for you anyway? Had my eye on her last couple of days, when she was bike hopping… you know… man to man, but she never settled. Seems she's taken to you, so keep her. She's yours. Least I can do for not killing my crazy mate here. If she doesn't suit your needs, man like you, let me know. Plenty of tail round here. And while we are talking about things like that, let me show you our happy home!" Boise led Kane away towards the sheds.

Kane glanced back at Hunter who was still talking to the girl. At least they were together. He didn't want to get too separated from them though, just in case. "Mind if my friends join me?"

"Later. Just want to show you something," and Boise led him away.

That made Kane a little uneasy, not that he couldn't handle himself, but what did Boise want him to see that he couldn't show the other two? He had a good idea.

While Hunter was talking to Kel, he was keeping a close eye on Kane, who was never really out of his sight. He watched as Boise and his new friend were joined by a couple of guys from the house. Boise and the two men shook hands like they had known each other for years. Boise then introduced Kane. The men he was introduced to looked older than the rest of the folks. Dressed in black and sporting short dark hair, they looked almost out of place. They were maybe Italian, maybe not. Hard to see from a couple of hundred feet away exactly who they were. Definitely buyers.

"I think we should follow Kane. What exactly do you know about Boise and the rest of the guys here? Your department must be aware of what's going on. And who are the guys with them right now?" asked Hunter, still trying to focus on the men.

"Italian buyers, I think. My department has been looking for this place for months. They couldn't find it. Not surprised. It's very nicely hidden away in here. They sent men out as bikers, but they never got anywhere for some reason. Then they sent me… and promised me there would be a guy to help me out… My brother was a biker so it wasn't hard to pretend I was one." She was actually rather proud of the fact.

"So when you saw Kane, you thought he was your contact?"

"Something like that… but then I figured they wouldn't send the commander… so I thought maybe you were the contact, but you were too close to him. It all went down so fast, and if it's not either of you, then who is the contact?" She stood there in the darkness looking kind of like she was lost. She also reminded him of the other Kelly and knew it had to be very difficult for Kane.

Hunter blinked. Suddenly, he had lost sight of his boss. Not good.

"You wanna take a walk with me? I can't see Kane…" Hunter was straining his eyes to see him.

He sensed her hesitation. "I assure you, you are quite safe with me… with Kane, I am not so sure …" and he made an attempt at a laugh about the subject. "Seriously, let's go find him."

She slipped her arm in his. "Where were they heading?"

"He and Boise were going towards the sheds accompanied by the guys in black. See if we can catch up to them. Good guess as to what's in there!"

"Yeah, me, too! The department thinks it's either heroin or cocaine. I am sure your boss knows what it looks like, right?" She clung onto Hunter's arm now, feeling quite safe in doing so.

"First hand!" he said, rather too quickly.

"Really, that's surprises me," she retorted.

"Forget I said that. It's a long story, connected to his wife's death. Speaking of which… is your name really Kelly?" He had to ask.

"Yes, why? Oh, Agent Branson, his wife. I saw the write-up for the funeral in the paper last week." She paused. "My god, you don't think Boise has seen it, too, do you?" She turned ashen.

"I doubt he even reads the paper. If he has then our commander, as tough as he is, is a dead man walking!"

Chapter 23

It stank in the shed. Kane thought they had accidently walked into the toilets. The lighting was not much better than outside the shed until Boise turned on the light. The sight that greeted Kane was certainly not what he was expecting. His eyes adjusted to the electric lighting. Opposite were tables full of heroin. Hundreds of pounds of it. Kane gasped.

"Well, that's what you came for, right, Kane? Heroin?" Boise thought he was on the right track.

"Yeah, I came to buy!" retorted Kane.

"I knew it! That's why you stopped at the bar today. You have a boss close by?" Boise was more than overjoyed. He was right as usual and he also wanted to sell some of this for himself rather than his boss in Alice Springs who was making all the profit.

"Just a phone call away!" and Kane was thinking how fast he could get Sam there. Even though he looked like Kane, he was Asiatic and was once a drug kingpin, undercover that is. He would know exactly how to behave. "I better go call him. Get him out here." Out there was right, for several reasons. Kane was getting in just a little too deep and too fast. If he hadn't known better, he would have said this was all planned. But he had stopped at the bar; no one had made him do it! And only so many folk knew he was even leaving, let alone that he really wasn't going up the Gold Coast... unless they were being followed, or someone gave the location away. It wouldn't be Sam, and the only others that knew he was even taking the trip were his lawyer and Buchanan... and Sage and Dan. Maybe they had arranged for someone to follow him. Wouldn't be that hard for Dan to get that arranged, after all, he was an AFP agent...

It was then that Kane noticed someone in the corner of the filthy, rotting shed. There was a person tied to the chair, broken, bruised and bleeding. At the sound of voices, the man looked up. Kane recognized him immediately as a young agent who had transferred to the drug squad some months back. Now, he sat bound and gagged, with blood caked on the side of his face from a severe beating. His shirt was open, and black and blue bruises patterned his chest.

"You see him, Kane? He's a cop! And this is what we do to cops! We kill them!" He grabbed the agent's hair and yanked his head high so that Kane could get a better look.

Kane's blood ran cold. If the agent gave any signs of knowing him, they were both dead, but the agent was too far gone to recognize the commander.

"This part of your game too, huh? Cop killing?" Kane tried to remain calm.

"Yeah. Thought it might be yours, too, being a bounty hunter. Cops hate you for taking their jobs away and getting paid more than they do." Boise let loose with a cruel laugh and letting go of the hair, let the head fall onto the young man's chest. "Hey, you want to take a turn?" and implied Kane could also beat up on the cop.

"Trying to give it up, even though they are the scum of the earth," and turned his attentions to the heroin instead. "Good stuff? Clean cut and pure?" It was all he could think of at that moment to distract Boise. Kane also noticed the two Italians who were standing very close to the door as if guarding their deal.

"You wanna test it out? Feel free. As you can see there is plenty of it." Boise pulled an already open bag across the table to Kane. Several syringes lay on the table. If heroin wasn't on the menu, aids was.

"Trying to give that up, too. As you probably saw by my arms, I've done enough of that crap for now," and Kane knew he couldn't touch the stuff or he would be right back to where he was in Japan... addicted. "You got any alcohol in this dump? That's what I need..." 'The word need was right,' thought Kane. "That and the woman out there..." 'Crap line and you know it,' thought Kane, but it sounded good. "My friend outside has both. Maybe I should go join him. I might be missing out on something... you know, they may start without me!"

"Sure. Anything you want. I could use a woman myself. Let's come back here later and discuss payment..."

There it was. Payment. Kane had a good idea that it involved cop killing. He had to get Sam there and fast. Kane moved to the door and with some sort of signal from Boise, the two Italians let him through. He smiled at them and all he got back was a glare.

"Nice night for a walk, mate," he muttered as he passed on by them to his friends. "And where the fuck have you two been? Big help there, *Hunter*. I could be dead by now!" The emphasis was on Hunter. "Oh, and don't let *her* go in there!"

"Why? Why shouldn't I?" she asked rather loudly, her pink lips pursing.

"'Cause, there is someone in there that might know you, darling, and I don't think you could handle it if they did!" and with that Kane took off back to the Harleys and the hipflask on Hunter's bike.

"Is he always that rude and arrogant?" 'Willowy' asked, turning round to look at the vanishing Kane.

"Mostly... especially with new folks. You get used to it. I should go after him. You coming?" and Hunter took off after Kane knowing the girl would follow.

"Yes," and she knew better than to leave them and be on her own. Obviously, Kane knew much more than he had told them.

At Hunter's Harley, Kane rescued the hipflask. There wasn't much scotch left, and it was gone in two seconds. "You have a bottle hidden in your clothes?" he mumbled, and Kane proceeded to rifle through his bodyguard's clothes. He found the bottle like he knew he would, knowing he could always rely on Hunter. He pulled it out of its hiding place and stuck it in his jacket. By this time the other two had joined him.

"Found it then, Kane? Then again, I didn't hide it that well!" Hunter moved to his bike and repacked the clothes. "Good job I didn't have money stashed in there. So, what was in that shed, aside from drugs?"

"Heroin… and a cop! A half-dead one who can give us and the girl away…" he stopped as 'Willowy' had now joined them. "He certainly knows me… Boise asked me if I wanted to take a turn beating up on him."

"What?! What did you say?" Even Hunter was amazed at this.

"Told him I was trying to give it up," and laughed. But it was a weird laugh, like he didn't believe what he had just been shown, and also what he had just said. He leaned very close to Hunter. "I think… I think somehow we were followed here or we were supposed to be here… something, I don't know. But we are where someone wants us to be. And Sam… I have to get Sam here. He can play drug lord again. Boise wants to meet *my* boss!"

"Kane, slow down! You're not making sense. How much did you drink today? Who followed us? Sam?" All the questions came out at one go.

"No, not Sam. Need Sam. I think Dan may have had us followed, which means other folks know we are not on our way to Brisbane and that's not good, especially now."

"Why not now, Kane? What are you not telling me… the call… it was from Sam, right? The last call you had… it's something to do with Reese, right? Kane… out with it. Is she still missing?" He realized he wasn't getting through to Kane. "Is she dead?" Hunter was very demanding to his boss and his voice was very raised.

"What the fuck you asking me for? And stop yelling at me like that! I'm your…" and Kane realized what he was about to say. He stopped, thinking that anyone close by would hear him.

A small group of Boise's bikers were already staring at him and actually seemed to like the conflict, hoping for another fight. They had already seen what Kane could do and started to circle round the three cops.

"Because I know you! You remove what's in your way! You have since I have known you. You don't need me, Kane! You never have! You are a one-man demolition squad." Now, it was Hunter's turn to yell and be heard to yell.

"Then get the fuck out of here, mate! You are right! What do I need a *man* like you for!" He grabbed at 'Willowy' and got hold of her arm pulling her to him. "Now her… I could really take to her." He leaned his head down and nestled into her soft, blonde hair. It smelled good, just like she did. "Think 'Willowy' and I should get to know each other a whole lot better in the next few hours." He rose up and looked Hunter straight in the eyes. "And you, you should find *your friend*, right? Maybe call him and invite him over while I go and enjoy myself. So, mate, I bid you farewell… for now!"

"Glad to go, to be honest. You are a pain in the ass, Kane! Don't bother to call me. I will be too busy on my phone to answer you… with my friend Sam!"

"Fuck you!" and Kane turned his attentions very obviously to Kelly, his free hand sliding all the way down her backside.

Kane was safe for now. He had a cop with him, even if the girl hadn't a clue what was going on, and if they had been followed, Hunter would find out by whom and get rid of the evidence… one way or the other. That was his job.

Hunter climbed onto his Harley, looked back one time at Kane and the girl, and then high tailed it out of the ranch at breakneck speed to do exactly what Kane had just told him to do.

Chapter 24

Hunter kept going out of the gates and onto the highway. It was now pitch dark and he had his headlamps on. It had been one hell of a long day that wasn't getting any easier, and he was very tired. Twenty or so miles down the road, he stopped the Harley and pulled out his mobile phone. He and Kane had left an unintentional trail behind them simply because no one, except Sam, was supposed to know where they were going.

Hunter dialed the operator and obtained the number for both the petrol station and the bar. He got both places on the first call. Fortunately, the kid with Kane's business card was still on duty. He remembered Hunter, actually Kane, and told Hunter that someone else had come through there some three hours back asking about the two men with long hair and they had described them very accurately. The call to the bar proved the same. Only the bar keep had not told the tail where to find the ranch. Someone else on Boise's payroll, but at least it would take the person longer to find them. All Hunter had to do was go back down the highway some more, and wait. A lone biker at this hour should be easy enough to spot. Now he had to call Sam, and this was something he did not look forward to. He couldn't help wondering what Kane was up to at this point in time.

Hunter dialed Sam's mobile number. As he did, he could see a motorcycle on the other side of the road. It slowed down and pulled onto the side of the highway. Not a very smart thing to do in this lighting. The rider pulled his mobile phone from inside his jacket.

"Hello..." His voice was hesitant, not recognizing the number.

"Sam? Is that you across the street? Is it? Did you just slow down on the highway?"

"Hunter? Where are you… I see a Harley across the way… is that you? Where's my father? Is he okay?" Sam looked across the median strip.

"Yes, to both questions. Hold on and I will come over to you. Stay right there!" Hunter put his mobile away and started the engine of his bike. He crossed the center strip and rode down to Sam's Harley, pulling alongside him.

The men shook hands, both fast and firm grips. Sam undid his helmet and pulled it off, hanging it from the handlebars.

"Glad you are here, Sam. Kane needs you!" Hunter spoke first.

"I can imagine…"

"No, you can't! You have to play the drug lord again like you did in Hong Kong!" He said, while screwing up his face in mock gesture.

"What?! I was trying to give that up!" Sam answered, laughing.

"Now, where have I heard that today? Only thing is, I don't think you can come in on a Harley… and where did you get that anyway?" Hunter stared closer. It was Kane's spare machine. "He has nice expensive rides, doesn't he? But that's not gonna do it… we need to get you a car and a driver." Hunter stopped, mainly because he was dead beat.

"You okay, Hunter? You look tired, mate."

"I am… very… isn't there a small hotel back down the highway? I seem to remember it on the left hand side… and don't you need to rest as well? You've been on the road the same length of time, more or less…"

"I am bushed, and you are right. Wasn't very big, but it did have a vacancy sign outside. Will Kane be okay for the night, wherever he is?" Sam was looking up the highway.

"Oh, yeah. Your father is just fine. He has a girl with him, albeit she is a cop aged somewhere between sixteen and twenty-six!" replied Hunter, sarcastically.

"Seriously? How in god's name did he manage that? No… don't answer that one. Better I don't know! I thought you would be much further on than this. Where is he anyway? I can't imagine you would be too far away from him."

"Never, but tell me… why did you come after us? He said you called him… and, yes, we should be in Adelaide by now. But he stopped at a bar!" Hunter looked a little frustrated.

"I did call him. Reese is missing… I called Kane and told him not to come back. And, yes, before you tell me… I know he left the house last night on his own. Star saw him."

"Dear god! Who else? I hope not Dan or Sage, because for some reason, whether they are your kin or not… I don't trust them anymore." Hunter said the last statement with some reservation. He was talking about Sam's stepsister and her husband.

"No… they don't know, only me and Star, and she isn't going to say a word. I told her where I was going, so at least someone knows, and again, she isn't going to tell them. Step-sisters they may be, but they are nothing alike." Sam leaned down on his Harley. He was tired. He shook his head. "So you want to tell me the rest… let's drive back down the highway and get rooms… then you can fill me in. Maybe we can also get a car service for tomorrow. Whatever you think is the right way to do whatever we are going to do."

"Good idea. Kane is about twenty-five miles up the highway. I know what I am supposed to do, call you and get you here. Didn't quite bank on you getting here this quick, so we have to leave him the night anyway. I am sure he can find something to do… they have a lot of alcohol, girls and heroin!"

"The last bit doesn't sound too good…"

"Don't worry. He isn't about to touch it… the girl, maybe he might. He's *your* father! And to make things worse, her name is Kelly!"

"Seriously? What were the chances of that? Please don't tell me she looks like her?"

"In some ways. She is blonde, taller than your step-mother was. Same kind of clothes, though, and the heels. Sometimes carries a gun, rides Harleys… and she's an AFP cop. She likes Kane… then what woman doesn't?" Hunter laughed. In a weird kind of way he envied Kane.

"So, he's set for the night! Is he carrying?" asked Sam.

"Yes. We both are and he has his mobile switched on. We can leave him a message so that he knows where we are. I assume you have your gun? Or at least, one of Kane's guns?"

"Yep… borrowed one of his." Sam patted the back of his pants. "Took a .357 for good measure. He is hardly going to miss it. Whole damn house is full of them. But I do think we should get rooms and something to eat. Decide how to play this and let him know the plan." As Sam spoke he took the helmet off the handlebars and put it back on his head. "You and dad ever wear them?"

"Nope. Never. Not part of our uniform," and Hunter revved the throttle on his bike. "You know... the one we don't have!"

They took off back down the highway, both zero to eighty in the same seconds. Kane had taught them both well. Two dots on the horizon heading back towards Sydney and the hotel.

The vacant sign still hung there, and flashed with garish lighting, 'Vacancy'. They were able to procure two rooms next to each other on the second floor. It wasn't the best hotel in town, but it wasn't the worst either. The only food they could obtain were snacks from the vending machine, the kitchen was closed. So, peanuts, chocolate chip cookies, crisps, and some fruit bars were dinner, washed down with lemon and lime sodas. Not the healthiest, but at least filling.

They sat in Sam's room. Sam perched on the end of his patchwork-quilted bedspread, and Hunter on the hard-backed chair, leaning on the table. He thought if he didn't, he would fall asleep. Hunter filled Sam in on the rest of the day. The knife fight, the girl, and the heroin shed. Hunter thought that was enough for Sam to take in right now.

Sam was trying to piece everything together that had happened in the last forty-eight hours from the funeral to now. How did the bikers find Kane? Someone else knew where he was going and someone tipped them off as to where he would be. But still, how did they know exactly how to make contact with him? Unless the same someone had called ahead and the bikers were supposed to find him, not the other way round. He shared these thoughts with Hunter. Two men, so very opposite, except a few months apart in age, worried about another man... one they both cared about.

Sam knew Kane was normally a very strong man both physically and mentally. But he wondered right now could he really cope with all this. He should have come with him. Yet again, he wasn't there for his father. And, yet again, Hunter was.

Chapter 25

The ranch was a total hubbub of activity. More bikers joined the fray and Boise arranged for cases of beer to be distributed amongst them. Kane took a couple of bottles along with his scotch and he and 'Willowy' headed for the nearest quiet place. They were few and far between. The house seemed the only place to go with its many rooms, including six or seven bedrooms. They found a small one at the very end of the hall. Kane had opened the door, and, thinking it was not occupied, ushered the girl into it. She almost but fell through the doorway and landed on the rather dirty looking bedcover. Kane closed the door behind him, switching on the light as he did and locked the door. Lighting proved the room was dirty, but habitable. There was one bed, an old whicker chair and washbowl. Kane thought it looked like something from a western movie set. Once, very nice and bright paintings of landscapes hung on the walls. Now they were dirty and dowdy looking. Curtains that matched the bedcover adorned the windows, but at least they had the room to themselves. Maybe they could get some sleep.

Kane was tired, the last few days catching up with him. He wanted to change clothes. He couldn't. His stuff was still on the Harley. The only things he had were his ID, credit cards, mobile phone, his gun… and the bottle of scotch. He was still in his leather, no shirt or sweater and he was cold. He needed the warmth of someone…

'Willowy' stared around the room. She was on the only place to sit. The chair didn't look like it was habitable. She scrunched up on one corner of the bed and sat there, her knees tucked under her chin and her skirt not doing its job.

He could see her black lace underwear revealing a little more than it should. She slipped her high heels off very seductively and laid them on the cover.

Kane watched her. What did she think she was doing to him? He could see her body quite clearly. The only thing missing from the low cut T shirt was Kelly's butterfly tattoo. How he missed that. How he missed his Kelly. He sat down on the edge of the bed, his eyes taking in her young body. And how he wanted sex… but not with her, with Kelly, and how he knew that was never going to happen again. Never make love to his wife again… He couldn't stand it…

"Get out! Get out of this room, NOW," and he immediately stood up and backed towards the window, bottle still in his hands. He was shaking and his voice was very loud.

"What?" 'Willowy' was terrified of him. "I can't go out there! What's wrong with you, Kane?" She pulled herself up to the bedrail and clung to it. His moods were as fast as his speed on the road.

"One more chance… get out of the bedroom, lady. I need…" and he shook his head from side to side.

This time she got the picture. "Kane… if that's what you need…" and pulled her T shirt down on either side revealing the black bra straps that seemed to slip down with the shirt.

He looked at her. He couldn't believe she was offering her body to him. She hardly knew him except by reputation and one bike ride. Kane could not take his eyes off her. Why did she have to be called Kelly and why had he drunk so much… she was too much tempta- tion for him. All he had taken her there for was to talk about what to do. And apparently she had taken the idea the wrong way. And now he needed her. She was a junior undercover cop and he was the commander. Junior… who was he kidding! She was making a play for him. Drink a little more scotch and he wouldn't care.

"'Willowy'… you have a chance to make it in the force. Don't blow it by sleeping with me. I'm not worth it… and you don't know me. My daughter says I use women, and maybe she is right. I do, just to get what I need. Maybe I always have… And right now I need…" and Kane stopped, ashamed of himself. Sage was right all along even down to her own mother. The only woman he hadn't used for gain was his Kelly. It had always been easy for him to find a woman, even down to a shit hole like this place.

His thoughts were interrupted by a loud banging on the bedroom door.

"Kane, everything alright in there? Girl giving you grief? If she is, send her out and we will do a swap. You can have my girl. Kane?" Boise's voice was loud and very clear. "Kane? Open the damn door!" More banging on the door followed.

"Get your clothes off," Kane whispered to 'Willowy', as he took his leather off and dropped it on the bed.

Kane unlocked the door and stood framed in the doorway with 'Willowy' hanging off his arm just clad in black lace panties. Boise took a good look at her.

"Damn. Should have taken her when I could. Mind if I have her after you?" His eyes never left her body.

"Yeah. I mind. She's too good to let go…" and Kane hit her on the backside. "Now, if your girl wants to join us, that's different…" Kane knew that wouldn't fly.

"Think I'll keep her," but Boise looked annoyed. "Oh, nearly forgot… brought you something," and he handed Kane a joint.

"Trying to give it up!" and Kane refused it.

"Come on, Kane… not sociable to turn down a smoke with us. Right, Kel?" and he handed it to 'Willowy' instead.

Kane interceded. "Well, if you put it like that…" and Kane took a couple of drags on it knowing full well it would increase his heart rate. Just what he didn't need. "Not bad. Had better," he lied.

"So you two staying in here the night?" Boise questioned, while hugging his own girl to him as if to make a point. His girl was no 'Willowy'. Fatter and not such a great figure. Long dark hair and a couple of teeth capped in gold.

"Thought we might. Been a few weeks for me… you know… thought I might spend a few hours catching up…" Kane felt a buzz.

"I'll be in the next room if you change your mind about swapping," Boise added, while he took the joint back from Kane. "Bang on the wall if you change your mind, mate."

"Right. I'll remember. I'll be banging but not for you," laughed Kane and ran his hand round 'Willowy's' shoulder and down onto her young breast. He felt her react instantly. And now a chance for her to escape was gone. He had touched her and now he wanted her.

Boise could see the look in Kane's eyes. Kane wasn't going to let the girl go now and that wasn't in the plan. He wanted the girl, but to upset Kane wouldn't help him too much. Kane was a killer and it oozed from every pour of the man. He could also use him to buy his drugs, make some money on the side and get paid well... sweet deal, unless it went wrong. So best to keep him happy. He still had no idea that Kane was a cop, nor did he know that Kel was. Bounty hunter, yes, cop, no. If he had known about Kel, she would have been sitting next to her friend in the heroin shed.

"So... if that's all you wanted to tell me, I will get to business," and Kane pushed the door a little further into the frame. "See you in the morning, and by then my boss should be on his way here."

"Right, mate. Australian? European? What?"

"Wait and see... more of a surprise... and when that's done we go to on to Alice Springs, right? Places I need to be..." Kane was getting agitated.

"Sure. Tomorrow night latest. Maybe earlier. Okay, well I can see you are busy, so night, mate," and Boise finally walked away from the now closing door.

Kane closed the door and once more locked it.

'Willowy' still held onto him, his hand still touching her breast. She turned to him, her body on his.

"I gave you a way out. Why didn't you take it? Like I told you, I use women! Always have and always will. As long as you know that, and when we leave here, you will never see me again." He didn't believe he was saying that. It sounded like someone else speaking from inside him. That much scotch and smoking weed didn't slow Kane down, only enhanced his thoughts.

He led her back to the bed and with more force than was needed pushed her down on the quilt. He leaned over her looking into her eyes knowing this was totally wrong. Why didn't she stop him? Everything seemed to be going on in a blur. It had been a long time since he had combined alcohol and weed. A very long time. Back in his teens.

'Willowy' lay under him. He was heavy on her.

"Kane, it's really okay…" and she pulled him closer to her

All Kane saw was Kelly, his Kelly.

"Kelly…" the only time he used her name, and his mouth closed on 'Willowy's' mouth and kissed her so passionately that she thought she would explode.

She had heard of his reputation… now she experienced it. There was no going back. She undid his jeans for him and reached inside them. Kane never wore underwear, never had. 'Willowy' was not surprised, nor was she surprised that her own underwear had disappeared without her realizing the fact. All she knew was that this man was all that she had heard… and a hell of a lot more.

Chapter 26

When 'Willowy' cried out, Kane covered her mouth with his hand, but he made sure that Boise heard her through the wall first. He wasn't so far gone that he didn't know what he was doing.

"Fuck!" Boise whispered. "That wasn't supposed to happen!" and he thumped his hand on the wall. He really had had plans for Kel.

Boise laid there, his girl asleep now. He heard 'Willowy' again at least twice more.

"God damn him! Doesn't he need a break?" and he turned over in the bed and put a pillow over his head, realizing it had been a bad move to take the room next to Kane. He slid off the bed and pulled his mobile from his jeans pocket, flipped it open and made the call.

"Yeah, it's me. Everything is fine to the point where he is still here. You sure he's a bounty hunter? Yeah, yeah, you said." There was a long pause. "You'll be here tomorrow, right? He's anxious to keep going. Occupied? Course he is! Been in the next room with some girl most of the night. Doesn't sound like he will be leaving her anytime soon either... judging by..." Boise paused. "Hey, I can't help it if the guy has a high sex- drive... or right, I hear you!" and he flipped the mobile shut. "Not getting paid enough to do this crap!" and he sat back down on the bed and thought about sleep.

The rest of the house was quiet now, even Kane's room. It was almost three a.m. Boise lay back on the bed. He should have asked for double the money. He was tired of working for other folks. His boss took most of the heroin money and when his old friend had called him and offered him several grand in cash to do a job, he had jumped at the chance. All he had to do was stop Kane from reaching Alice Springs... couldn't be that hard, or could it? Kane was no ordinary man. Boise couldn't put his finger on it, but there was some piece of the puzzle that was missing. Something the person on the phone had not told him. Why didn't they want Kane in Alice Springs? Now his own curiosity was raised after he had met the man. And where had his partner gone after such a violent argument? More questions.

In the next room, Kane lay back on the pillows. What he had just done was not right, both for the girl and for his health. He pulled his jeans back on trying not to wake the sleeping 'Willowy'. He watched her for a moment… no, it wasn't right and it wasn't going to happen again. Remembering his mobile, he pulled it from his pants pocket. Normally it lived its life in his boot, but that didn't seem the correct thing to do when riding a Harley. There were a couple of missed calls. He moved nearer the window, out of earshot, and listened to the messages. Both were from Hunter telling him that Sam was here and they were about thirty miles away at a motel and could he somehow call them back. If he couldn't, then they planned to get a car and come in the morning to buy drugs. Hunter had explained how Sam had followed them and who else knew and their theories about the Angels wanting to keep him there.

He pulled his boots back on and this time Kane did put the phone in his boot. Maybe it was safer there. He retrieved his leather from the floor where he had dropped it in haste, sat down on the bed next to the girl and gently shook her. She stirred slightly, her eyes flickering as she focused on his face. He moved his feet slightly and kicked the empty bottles on the floor. Just another reminder of a night that should not have been, and yet as he looked at 'Willowy' he wanted more. Standing up, he pulled the quilt around her.

"We need to get downstairs. Don't know about you, but I am hungry." 'Oh geez, that was lame!' Kane was amazed at his own stupidity.

"What time is it?" she asked, looking into his face, not quite sure what day it was.

"Eight. You have clothes around here somewhere," and he began searching for them. He found them in some odd places, and handed them over. "There has to be a bathroom round here. Even Angels have to pee," and he laughed, very uncertain of himself.

"Do we have to go out there? I don't trust those guys…" she looked concerned.

"'Willowy'… there is something you should know. In the shed… well, there is a young cop that I think I am supposed to kill…" There was no other way than to be direct with her now. They were not just travelling companions, but lovers. He waited for her to either yell at him or to burst into tears. She did neither, just stared at him like she did not believe him.

"Why didn't you tell me that last night? Why now? You think that was going make me betray you or something? I wouldn't do that, sir, and I certainly don't think you would kill him." Her eyes were very big, just like silver dollars. Innocent…

Kane pondered a moment. He hadn't said what sex the person was. He thought about stating his thoughts out loud and decided against it. Had he just slept with a traitor? Now he wasn't sure, but better to keep her near him just in case. He dreaded to think what Sam was going to think… and Hunter.

A loud banging on the door disturbed his thoughts.

"Kane… Kane… some guy at the gate says he is your boss. Asiatic guy in a big car. You know him?"

"Yeah, I know him," Kane yelled back through the door. He turned to look at 'Willowy', who was pulling on clothes as fast as possible.

She nodded to Kane that she was dressed and he opened the door. Boise peered in the room, taking in everything he could. 'Willowy' moved in behind Kane and stood there waiting to see what happened next. She whispered in Kane's ear. He nodded.

"You have a bathroom round this place, Boise? She needs one," and inclined his head back at her.

"End of the landing. You want help finding it, Kel?" Boise asked, wiping his fingers across his mouth and leering intently at her.

"Yeah, she does… from me!" and Kane took hold of her hand and led her down the hallway, leaving Boise standing watching the pair.

In the morning light the bathroom was easy to find. The door didn't shut into the frame. No wonder Boise wanted to go with her. 'Willowy' went inside and Kane stood in front of the partially open door, so that no one else could see her. He hoped she would do the same for him. She did. He wished there was time to wash, but looking at the basin it needed it more than he did. He pulled his hair back in a band after trying to comb it with his fingers which did not work out too well. He stuck his hand inside his leather to make sure that his pills were still there. While doing so, he retrieved his silver K that normally hung round his neck. Tucked behind it was his Kelly's K. He looked into the dirty, cracked mirror that hung over the sink, rubbed it clean with his sleeve so that he might see his face.

"I said no matter what happens, Kel," and he hung both K's back round his neck, one much tighter than the other one. He also made sure that his gun was ready and able, in the side of his jeans, should the time come to use it.

"You say something, Kane?" 'Willowy' whispered to him from outside the open door.

"No. Be right with you. Stay there. Wait for me…" He finished up and was thinking about going to meet his son, and hoping that Sam didn't say anything he shouldn't.

"You bet your life I will," and she looked up and down the landing. People were moving, drunken, doped. Who knows what they were doing? She certainly had no intention of going anywhere now without Kane.

Finally, he emerged from the bathroom and the first thing she saw past his open leather were the K's. "Both yours?"

"Yeah," and taking her hand, led her down the creaking stairs and out into the main room. "Still hungry?" Kane asked her, glancing around the room. It was sparsely furnished, just well-worn chairs and the odd table. Drab curtains hung from a couple of the windows in an attempt to block out the fast approaching brilliant rays of sunlight.

"A little… I can see fruit over there on the table. Shocked they would even know what fruit is in this place!"

"Me too… there is a bottle of scotch there also. Grab the apples, and the scotch, and let's go meet my boss," replied Kane.

"You are…" and 'Willowy' stopped dead as Kane nearly squeezed her hand off her arm. "I'll get the fruit…" and she broke away from him.

He watched her very carefully, a frown on his face. He glanced round the room. No one seemed to have heard her. They were mostly screwed up bikers who still had not joined the day. He watched as she grabbed a couple of apples, the scotch and a giant bag of crisps that someone had left there from last night. Waiting for her by the main door, Kane pulled the band from his hair, realizing it wasn't really the macho image to have his hair tied back. Now to go meet his son, the ominous Asiatic buyer, by the gate.

He and 'Willowy' were out the door ahead of most of the folk and Boise stood waiting almost impatiently, as Kane and his girl opened the bottle. Kane had a couple of gulps, and ate half the apple. Sam could wait… then, again, maybe that was showing disrespect to his *boss*.

"Okay, lady… now you get to meet my *boss*…" and Kane moved forward towards Boise and joined him, walking at a fairly good pace towards the waiting car.

Boise wasn't sure who this was. All he knew was he could make some more side money. Kane might be the bounty hunter, and someone was stopping him, for some reason, going to Alice Springs. But Kane seemed to have connections and one of them was climbing out of a very expensive car.

Sam stepped out of the driver's side, but left the engine running. Next to the car Hunter sat on the Harley, both legs on the same side of the bike, watching and waiting, his gun very reachable. They both stared at Kane as once again he swaggered towards them, the girl hanging off his arm, occasionally whispering in his ear. Both men knew where Kane had spent the night, and both men were not that pleased with him, and Kane knew it. All it did was made him more arrogant… if that was possible.

"Boise… I would like you to meet *my boss*… Mr. Cheng… he is the nephew…" and Kane paused so slightly that Boise would not have caught it, "of the infamous Vau Cheng from Hong Kong, drug dealer second to none!"

Chapter 27

Kane didn't flinch. He looked his son in the eyes and stood there like he owned the place. Sam stared back, not so much at Kane, but at the young girl with him. Was this man really his father? He was beginning to wonder. He knew what Hunter had told him and he also knew that Boise thought Kane was a bounty hunter. Apparently his father was living up to that creed and then some. The girl was still draped around his shoulders, and he had his arm round her waist just touching her skirt, if one could call it that.

Mr. Cheng was not what Boise was expecting, and he had a couple of his blokes with him as he moved from Kane to the drug dealer. He wiped his hand on his pants leg and stuck it out to Sam, who stared at the hand and looked back into Boise's face. He had no intention of shaking his hand or anyone else's.

Sam Cheng-Branson was dressed from head to toe in black. His blonde hair was tucked under a black hat that hid most of it, and his demeanor was totally different than usual. Kane thought he looked more like the day he had met him in the night club in Hong Kong. Kane knew Sam could pull it off with Boise, but he also knew that Sam's furious looking expression was mainly due to him. Kane took another step forward.

"Nice car, boss. Not seen this one before…" On the edge, that's where Kane lived. Right on it!

"Kane," Sam was curt. "This worth my while, or one of *your* side ventures?" His more than British accent was still strong from all the years spent overseas in schools there.

"Good stuff, boss. You know I only find that. Over there in the shed." Kane inclined his head towards the building where the cop was, all the time telling his son far more than Boise knew. "Mr. Boise here will show you... See you came back then, Hunter? Miss me?" and Kane laughed out loud and turned back towards 'Willowy'.

"Mr. Cheng, let me show you the heroin... pure cut and no middle man." Boise was salivating at the mouth. Suddenly, he could see money for himself, and a lot of it. In the back of his mind, he wondered why his phone friend wanted Kane stopped. Kane seemed like one of them... tough and on the wrong side of the law. Maybe he should have asked for more details. Too late now. "You wanna go take a look?"

Sam tipped his head, just slightly and moved towards him. Hunter stayed exactly where he was.

Kane whispered to 'Willowy'. "You have anything you need to get? Purse, ID? Anything?"

"No. I stashed it on your Harley when you weren't looking. Just a small purse in with your stuff. It's only a false ID, credit card... and some underwear." She tweaked her hair with her fingers and pursed her mouth for effect, wishing right now she had the gloss that was on the back of the Harley.

"Oh, wonderful... when on earth did you do that?" He asked her, very much surprised.

"When I climbed on the bike. Don't worry. I hid it well," and she looked very satisfied with herself.

"Since when do I wear underwear? Let alone ones like yours?" Kane stated fairly loudly, meant for the other bikers to hear.

Hunter heard. His face narrowed in anger. Was this all a game to Kane? The guys round Kane laughed, and even at this hour had bottles of beer in their hands. Then again, Kane was carrying a bottle of scotch and, if Hunter was right, not the same one from last night.

Kane tipped the bottle to his mouth and took a couple of gulps. He watched Sam from the corner of his eye move down the path towards the sheds. He also knew Hunter was watching him. Before they could do anything, they needed to get the young cop out. He was a sitting target... one that Kane figured he was supposed to take care of.

"Hey, boss..." yelled Kane. "You need some help in the shed?"

"Yes, Kane. Just you..." replied Sam.

Kane whispered to 'Willowy', who let go of him and sidled over to Hunter. She whispered in his ear and perched herself against him. Now Hunter knew what Kane was doing. He glanced to the left of him and could see Kane's ride. "Kel, is he okay? I mean physically..." He didn't quite know how to phrase it. He could hardly say 'was he okay after sex last night'? Or 'did you really have sex with Kane'?

"He's fine, why?" and there was a puzzled look on her face like she hadn't a clue what he was talking about.

"Just don't... well, just don't mess with his feelings right now... you know what I am saying?" Hunter was trying to be as nice as he could.

"Because of his wife... or something else?" she asked tentatively.

"Couple of things. His wife is one... and another thing. But if he hasn't told you, then I can't... you plan on seeing him after this is over?" Hunter really wanted to know.

"Think that's between him and me..." She looked at Hunter's serious face. Maybe not a good thing to lie to his partner and very obviously his bodyguard. "No. He made that very clear last night. It was just a one-night stand. I was just someone that fulfilled his needs..." She said the last part with some remorse.

"Seems Kane is good at that..." Hunter looked down at his own Harley, but he also noted Kelly's voice.

"You say something?" she asked, knowing full well what he had said and suddenly she felt just a little bit cheap.

"Go sit on his Harley, and Kelly, be ready, just in case! I think I know what Kane is doing." At least he thought he knew.

"Glad one of us does... the Asiatic man with him... he looks a little like K..." She didn't get to finish and was staring after Sam like she had figured something out.

"Right! Now go to his bike and stay there whatever happens, unless he or I call you... you get my drift?" Hunter paused. "You carrying?"

"Do I look like I am?" She ran her hands down her body. There was nowhere to hide a gun.

"Guess not, no." He reached to the back of his bike, pulled out his own spare gun and made sure it was loaded. "Here... Now there are four of us." He hesitated as he watched her looking at the firearm. "You do fire guns in your branch of the AFP, right?"

"Very cute..." and she took it from him. "Just where am I supposed to hide it?" 'Willowy' commented, as she again looked down at her body.

"His Harley... go...!"

This time she went leaving Hunter staring at her. "Dear god... why does he do it? Like some sort of death wish. He's gonna damn well die on the job!" He shivered, realizing just what he had said.

She leaned against the Harley and made sure her things were still well hidden in Kane's clothes. Her purse was cloth and blended nicely with his black T shirts. Now she hid the gun, but not too far in, just enough so she could grab it when the time came. She hadn't answered Hunter. She was actually a crack shot; something else that her brother had taught her, him and the Special Forces at the AFP. She was more undercover than even the commander knew and certainly more than she had told him. Kelly stood there thinking back to last night. She had heard of Kane and his reputation. She didn't think she would ever meet him. If anything he was her hero... and now she found he had feet of clay. But the memory of last night with him would always be hers, but just in case, she would leave him her number. Just in case...

"Kelly..."

She came back to her senses. "Yeah?"

"Stay alert!"

"I am, Hunter..." she tried to look like she wasn't day dreaming. But she was. She also knew that Kane was waiting for something. Maybe it was the Asiatic gentleman, maybe it wasn't. He had mentioned to her, after they had made love, that he may need help in Alice Springs. That he was looking for something or someone and perhaps she would be up to helping him. In fact, he had told her a lot, now she thought back. Kane had told her what he wanted her to know so that she would help him, and he had almost prostituted himself last night because he knew that's what she wanted and at that time, so did he.

Chapter 28

Boise switched the light on in the shed. Sam stepped inside along with Kane. He moved to the left and the first thing Kane noticed was that the young cop just hung there, still tied to the chair, head down on his chest. Kane knew instinctively he was dead. Sam turned his head slightly to his right and could see the anger rising in his father's face. It was red and his eyes became slits. Hunter had told him there was a cop in the sheds and now it was too late to help him. Kane took a step forward and, instinctively, Sam went to stop him.

"Kane… you were going to show me the stuff…" and Sam steered him in the opposite direction from the dead cop. "Not yet, Kane…" whispered his son. "Your chance will come… soon," he whispered, and then he changed course. "*Mr*. Boise. Show me what you have. If it's good, I will give you cash. Mr. Kane here can verify it for me. He is good at his job and very reliable."

"So I heard…" and Boise corrected himself, "and I saw how he handled himself yesterday!"

"Trouble, Mr. Kane?" asked Sam very quietly and almost serenely.

"No trouble, boss! Just reminded me of another time and place."

Sam knew exactly what he meant. Ryan Holden and Iraq sprung to mind.

"I heard about that, Kane. Didn't you cut the guy's heart out last time?" asked Boise, thinking about what Hunter had told him yesterday.

"Yeah, mate. I did. He was long overdue!" Kane said it with venom on his mind and fire in his eyes.

Boise shuddered. There was a strange look on Kane's face. Boise had seen it before when his own gang members were about to kill, and now he saw it again. Even for an Angel, he was a little nervous. He knew there was far more to the story then he had been told. He began to wish he hadn't taken the extra money for this job and also that the young cop in the corner was still alive, which reminded him… for a bounty hunter, Kane was awfully concerned, and then it struck him. Kane was not a bounty hunter… Kane was the bounty. That had to be it. That… or he was also a cop! If he was, he didn't look like any damn cop he had ever seen. Maybe he should call his contact again. Check to see how far away they were. Make sure the flight had landed. All kinds of things ran through his head. One of them being that Kane was one tough bastard and he wished he had brought a couple of guys in the shed with him. As if someone read his mind, the shed door opened and one of his more 'appealing' girls sauntered in.

"Want some food, Boise? Lady of the house is making some chili," and the long, black-haired girl chewed gum in her mouth, and then spat it out onto the floor.

A good reason to go outside… all of them!

"You like some food then?" His questioned was aimed at Mr. Cheng, but his eyes never left Kane.

"No, thank you. But I will step outside. The light in here is not good for my eyes. Kane… you said you think this is pure?" He was very direct.

"Yep, as driven snow." That was the truth. It was, but he wasn't sure if they were making it there on the property. But pure it was, and worth a hell of a lot of money. He could arrest Boise on this alone, plus murder of a cop. Whether he had killed the guy or not, he was still an accessory to the fact. But Sam was right. Now was not the time. Later was…

"Then we should discuss money. I am sure you have other buyers… like the Italians I saw outside… wouldn't that be right, Mr. Boise?" Sam was deliberately quiet and foreboding, hoping he was making the right impression.

"That's right, Mr. Cheng. But there is plenty to go around, as you can see. Let's step outside and see what you will offer me."

Sam nodded his okay and led the way out of the door, Kane behind him.

From where Hunter sat he could just see Kane and Sam. They were not more than large dots, but he could see them. When he couldn't, he was worried. If anything went wrong now they were way out numbered… three, no four of them against maybe thirty or forty Hells Angels and no one to call on for backup. Kane wasn't supposed to be there, he himself was undercover and so were Sam and the girl. Hunter wasn't nervous, just a little conscious of the fact they were much outnumbered, with the feeling that who ever planned this was also on their way here. He glanced at the girl. She seemed confident enough. She also seemed to have taken a shine to his boss and Hunter hoped that didn't cloud her judgment. She had pulled her purse from Kane's clothes and was glossing her lips. She ran a comb through her hair, then pushed the bag back on the bike and waited patiently for her lover to return.

Hunter almost felt sorry for her. She didn't deserve just to be discarded like some used doll. But he had to admit she had guts. She had survived a night with Kane and she was undercover with this lot of trash. He still could not figure out how old she was. The girl was good at hiding things… quite obviously.

Kane came back into good view, along with Boise and *Mr. Cheng*. Hunter had to admit Kane had been fast on his feet to call Sam by his old name. At least Sam had had the name for thirty-five years and would be totally used to it. Hunter liked Sam. It had been Sam that hadn't respected him, but now that was all changed, and he was glad.

Sam was doing most of the talking with Boise. Telling him how much he would pay for so many kilos of heroin, and then if it was good he would take more. Boise was rubbing his hands in glee, forgetting that he was supposed to be distracting Kane, but then again that was Kel's job. He hadn't loaned her out to Kane for no reason, even if she took to the job far more readily than he thought she would.

Kane walked slowly next to Sam, taking in everything that the two men were saying. While walking, Kane's eyes were scanning around him to make sure they were relatively safe. Feeling that they were, Kane took off back to his Harley. He noted that 'Willowy' looked very pleased to see him. Maybe he was being a little too hard on her by saying that she would never see him again. And maybe he should have thought of that last night.

"Miss me?" and he leaned forward, kissing her lips, just a fleeting glance of a kiss.

It took her by surprise and she responded eagerly to him, realizing her mistake.

"I guess you did," and Kane laughed almost a cruel laugh like a cat toying with a mouse. "Hunter give you a gun?" as his hand slid across the seat of the Harley towards the back of the motorcycle. He didn't let her answer. "I see he did!" and he touched the cold hard steel. He turned away from her just as though he had never touched her and walked to Hunter.

"Your daughter was right. You do use women, Kane!"

"Yep, I do…" and Kane laughed a cynical laugh. "I just hope to god that Boise sees that and the girl really does understand," and he turned away, looking at Sam and Boise negotiating the deal. Kane was being Kane… needing the upper hand as always.

As Boise approached looking exceedingly pleased with himself, Kane started on him.

"So we can leave now that my boss and you have reached an agreement? If you guys aren't for some reason, I am… and I think I might take the girl with me, you know, for fun." Kane had the feeling, for some reason, that they needed to get out of there. Head up the road a little and wait to see who showed up. He was beginning to put two and two together as to who was arriving. Who would gain by him not reaching Alice Springs? Only a couple of people. One was his own daughter, and her husband. The other was the so-called-mother of his new child. Someone who knew about his past maybe from a file. Someone who had access to that information… or maybe someone who could gain access… like lawyers. Whomever, he wanted out… and now. He wanted them all out. Seeing the dead cop made him realize that Boise and his merry band would stop at nothing, including killing AFP cops. And that probably included bounty hunters, even if they did bring in buyers for heroin.

Boise wasn't quick enough in his thoughts. "What's the hurry, Kane? You have all you want here… the girl, booze, dope… what else is there?"

"Freedom!" Kane came back at him. "I like the open road. Too confined here for me. I brought you a buyer. The cop is dead and you don't need my services anymore." He heard 'Willowy' take a breath and the wind in the trees, too, like they heralded some kind of death knell. Kane had meant to shake up the pot and now he had… maybe too much. He felt very uneasy, like he knew what was about to happen.

Sam took his cue. "I must be leaving, too. I have someone else to see today. I will send my men to you for the heroin and bring the agreed price in cash later this afternoon. Have the kilos ready near the gate and we will trade," and Sam stepped closer to the car. The engine sat idling. He had to take the car back and get Kane's other Harley away from the hotel before someone realized what was happening. He was so close, he and Kane, to leaving. Kane returned to his Harley and 'Willowy' was climbing on the back, when out of the shadow of the trees stepped a figure, someone no one was expecting to see.

Chapter 29

"What the fuck are you doing here?" asked Kane. He swung round to stare at the person, "and how long have you been standing there? You keeping tabs on me now and how the hell did you know where to look?" Kane blurted out the statements.

Dressed in dark jeans and black windbreaker, Ambassador Jenkins stepped into plain view. In his hand he held a rather bold looking gun, albeit it was down by his side. A .357 no less.

"Something like that, Kane... I have to make sure that *my wife* is taken care of... after all, she is leaving me for you, or so she thinks... Don't think she will be so happy about last night, though, with the young lady on the back of your Harley..." and Ambassador Jenkins laughed out loud. He sidled over to Boise. "You did a good job there, my friend." The dark haired, well-built American pulled a stash of money from his pocket and handed it to Boise. "You kept *him* here for me... no reaching Alice Springs for you, Kane. Not ever. In fact, no reaching anywhere else ever again. You see Boise here is working for me on the side... has been for some time. Never thought he might come in useful with *you* though. I am surprised, though, that you recognized me. I guess you have seen pictures or something after Iraq."

"Or something..." muttered Kane dismounting from the Harley and leaned against it.

"I do have to thank you, though, for getting Reese back for me. It would have been embarrassing to lose her over there, and thank you for killing Holden. He was a pain in all our sides. But you took care of him for us."

"Haven't you left someone out?" Kane raised his head high and looked directly at the Ambassador.

"Your wife? A casualty of war… but I understand a very pretty one… bit like the girl you screwed last night…"

That was too much for Kane and he made a move forward as if to punch out Ambassador Jenkins.

"Kane, no… the son-of-a-bitch isn't worth it. He will probably shoot you," 'Willowy' had jumped right in to defend the new man in her life.

"Let him shoot me," Kane mocked. "Wouldn't be the first time I've been shot and won't be the last! He hasn't got the guts!"

Boise looked from one to the other. "Am I missing some giant piece of the puzzle here, mates? Something I am not quite getting… Kane's a bounty hunter, right?" he asked Jenkins.

"Sure he is." Jenkins threw his arm round Boise's shoulders. "He kills terrorists for a living. Hired gun! Then you knew that, Boise. That's why you wanted him to kill your cop… but, Boise… didn't you know you have another one here also…" he laughed, totally full of himself and utterly confident.

"Cop or bounty hunter?" asked a confused Boise.

Now the Ambassador had to make a choice. He could give Kane away right then and be done with him, or he could just give the girl away. If he gave Kane away, it wouldn't be good for relations with the American and Australian Governments, and that he could not afford. He had only agreed with his soon to-be-ex to take Kane down… not to get him killed, tempting as it was, and he wasn't totally sure who was on whose side. He knew there were two men with Kane, but he had never seen them. Reese had not described Hunter or Sam, even though she had met them both in Iraq. She had just been thankful to be out of Holden's grasp. Kelly being killed was a bonus for her. How she had hated her and how she was manipulating her husband. Knowing how short of money her husband had become through gambling debts, and how rich Kane was, she had devised the plan with the Ambassador.

"Cop…"

Boise turned dead serious. "Which one and I will take care of the bastard right now…" and Boise pulled his own gun from the back of his filthy jeans, pointing in the direction of Kane, then towards Hunter and Sam. "One of these guys… has to be… I know all the rest…"

Jenkins thought so, too. But to denounce one of them would be to reveal Kane's identity.

"I was kidding, Mr. Boise. I think one bounty hunter is enough… you might want to keep the girl with you though… keep *our* boy here in check…"

"You touch one hair on her head and I will kill you!" Kane was positively venomous and pushed 'Willowy' behind him and to safety. "You understand me? If you, Mr. Jenkins, want to shoot me, that's fine… but you will not hurt her…" Kane could feel 'Willowy's' hands on the top of his jeans. He also knew where his gun was and could feel her hand heading that way round his waist, just in case. He also knew she had a gun on the back of his Harley, and that Hunter and Sam were both carrying. Still only them, though. He had hoped that Hunter would have brought back up or at least had them on standby, but he guessed not.

"Quite the tough guy, Mr. Kane. Reese said you were… that and much more. And quite the lover, I gather, and judging by the young girl with you today and a ten-year-old daughter named Leila, I would have to agree."

"Jesus Christ! For the last fucking time, that child is not mine, nor did I ever sleep with your wife, before or after you were married… whatever she told you!"

"Right, Kane… like you didn't sleep with Corey on the way to Iraq. You were married to Kelly then…" Jenkins laughed a very cruel laugh, like he was twisting the knife into Kane.

"I suppose your ever-loving wife told you that! She overheard that statement while I was disposing of Ryan Holden apparently for you and the American government. So what… I was drugged and why the fuck am I explaining this to you anyway? And it doesn't matter one jot to Reese. She would take me if I had slept with a thousand women… what's that like Ambassador… losing out to someone like me…?" Kane turned the tables nicely, positively gloating about the fact. "I have slept with more women than you have even thought about! Just ask all my children." And there it was said. All my children…

Neither Sam nor Hunter said a word. To do so would incriminate them both as police of some description and really Kane didn't need help. He was managing very well on his own. But they did glance at each other... children?

Jenkins glared at Kane. A big man, usually confident, had been demeaned in front of a gang of bikers by the man his wife was in love with, and now everyone knew. Jenkins was aware Kane was a clever man and that kind of man needed to be taken out. He glanced around. He figured that both he and the two men with him were armed. Probably the girl, too. Now was not the time to take Kane on, much as he wanted to kill him where he stood. It was then 'Willowy' spoke up, stepping in front of Kane as she spoke.

"Kane... I guess that makes me a thousand and one, two and three," and her laughter echoed round the Angels that had now gathered to watch the fray, hoping for a repeat performance from Kane just like yesterday.

Some of the Angels laughed and made a whooping-like sound egging her on. Whistling could be heard round the yard.

"And what's more, *my man* here," 'Willowy' said as loud as she could, "is one hell of a lover!"

Kane didn't know whether to hug her or strangle her. Probably a hug would be a good thing. He encircled her with his arms, whispering in her ear. "Leave me your number..."

She smiled.

"That satisfy you, Ambassador? Apparently, she was..." Kane pulled her even closer. "And what makes you think you can keep me here? You and whose army... And why can't you let me get to Alice Springs? Something there you don't want me to find out about? Maybe some people I shouldn't meet up with? Some Americans?" Slowly, it had been coming back to Kane. He had met a couple of girls there right after he came back from Nam. They had hung out for a month until one of them got into trouble with the police there and Kane had backed off from her. There had been parties and booze and sex... plenty of all three and Kane could handle all three. Just back from Nam, full of testosterone, free, and on his way home to see his grandparents... sowing wild oats. Maybe he had sown a few too many… but the girls were all his age. And then it hit him. Lewis had said relative… as in grandparent. Was Leila his grandchild? There was only one way to find out. Plow right in in front of the Angels and find the hell out.

Chapter 30

"So, then... my grandchild with you or Reese? You know, Leila? She is my granddaughter somehow, right?"

Jenkins looked totally staggered. "Don't be so stupid... how the hell could she be your grandchild when Reese is her mother?"

"Ah, but she's not, is she? And I am not the father. Father of someone in Alice Springs, maybe, but not Leila... did Reese find the child from somewhere? One that looks like me? I have to say she went to some length if that's the case." Kane was now quietly confident.

"Didn't you get the DNA results? Your lawyer has them... she has your goddamn DNA!" yelled Jenkins.

"So would my granddaughter." He looked at Jenkins. "She told you the child was hers when? How long ago did you know about the child, Ambassador? This year or last year? "

"Last year. She hid the child with her sister... she didn't want to upset our marriage." Jenkins was very agitated. His hand with the gun started to waver a little.

Kane started to laugh, all the time sliding his hand round the side of his jeans where his gun was. "Really... she told you after the child was nine? How convenient... And what did you think about that? Suddenly my child springs into your life. Was that about the time she thought about divorcing you, Ambassador? Or did that come later? Just curious, that's all..."

Hunter was carefully watching Kane. He knew that any minute his boss was going to pull his gun and quite possibly shoot an American with diplomatic immunity. He decided he should quite possibly leave his Harley and walk closer to Kane. Sam still stood by the open

159

car door, and he also had his hand on his gun, just in case.

If Jenkins had known Kane better, he would have realized he was pushing him. Kane had completely reversed the situation and now had the upper hand, both literally and figuratively. Kane was in control. Hunter wasn't sure if Boise completely understood what was going on, only that suddenly he didn't have as much control as he did before. Ambassador Jenkins had come in and stirred things up, and now Kane had taken over. Only thing Kane wished was that they had back up; little did he know that Hunter and Sam had actually called Buchanan and told him the situation.

"So, Ambassador... what's the next step? I know Reese is missing, and you probably think she ran off with me... well, news flash... she didn't... as the young lady with me can attest to. So, *sir*, where is she? Lurking in the bushes behind you? Hiding out somewhere till you blackmail me into paying you off? That isn't going to happen! Is she going to pop up any minute and say boo? You will never get a penny out of me now or forever! And now, I think I will be leaving to go and find my answers." Kane was positively obnoxious in his demeanor. He turned towards the Harley and pushed 'Willowy' ahead of him, out of the way, almost expecting the obvious.

Kane had walked several yards towards the Harley when he heard the click of the hammer on the .357 as it pointed at him. He turned, his gun in his hand, the killer, and he fired one shot. It hit Jenkins dead centre in his chest, even before he had time to pull the trigger. Jenkins stared into Kane's face, into his very soul, and slowly the gun slipped from his fingers, and, in slow motion, dropped to the earth beneath him.

No one moved. Kane's gun still sat rigid in his hand. The Ambassador clutched his hands to his chest and dark, red blood slowly oozed through his fingers. He looked down at his jacket, not believing he was shot and then back up at Kane. "Did you sleep with my wife...? I need to know..."

'Willowy' clasped her hands to her mouth to stop the scream in her brain reaching her lips.

Kane never answered him. He stood there not believing what he had done.

"Kane, lower the gun... Kane... give it to me... give me your gun..." and Hunter touched Kane lightly on his arm. Hunter retrieved the gun from Kane's hand and tucked it into his own jeans.

Boise stared from one to another. "You killed him... you fucking killed my friend... What the fuck did you do that for... ?" His eyes were wild, and his brain not believing what was happening. His bounty killer had shot someone alright... his friend and his bread and butter.

"The son-of-a-bitch was gonna kill him... didn't you see?" snarled Hunter.

"You shot him! Right out of the blue!" yelled Boise, and his sentiments echoed through the nearest member of the Angels.

"Are you blind, man? He had a gun in his hand..." Sam joined in. "I think maybe we should call the police..."

"No police, Mr. Cheng." Boise was quick to say it. "Okay, he had a gun, but he wasn't going to kill your man here!"

"And I wasn't going to wait to be shot in the back either..." Kane yelled back at him, and once more came back into the conversation. He leaned down on the ground and looked at Jenkins. He was still breathing, but barely. "He isn't dead! Someone needs to get him to a hospital..." and under his breath Kane commented, "and we need to get the fuck out of here before we are lynched!" He turned the Hunter. "Let's get out of here... now!"

"Agreed..." and he handed Kane back his firearm.

Sam left the car where it still idled. As Hunter climbed on the Harley, Sam took the seat behind him. Kane made for his own machine and on the way grabbed 'Willowy's' hand.

"Let's go, Missy. They will be on us like a pack of wolves."

"But it was fair..." 'Willowy' stated, turning to look at the seemingly very pissed of Boise. "You would be dead if you hadn't fired first..."

"They don't think so... let's go... unless you want to stay with your friends here and end up like Jenkins or worse..." Kane peered into her face.

'Willowy' shuddered. "No thanks... where you go, I go..." and she kept pace with him to his ride.

Kane climbed on the bike, waited till she was on behind him and handed her his gun. "Here! If you have to, use it... none of us want to die right here." To him that was a strange thought. Maybe it was best if he did die there. Solve a lot of problems. He shook his head. His mind needed to be clear and it wasn't. He revved the bike, turned to her. "Let's get the hell out of here! You secure?"

"I'm fine... go, Kane!" and with one arm she clung to him. In her other hand she held the gun at her side.

The two Harleys took off at breakneck speed, out of the gate and onto the open road. They turned sharply back towards Sydney and the hotel, Hunter leading the way with Kane closing the gap. Two motorcycles blazing a trail... and a very fast one. Even above their party's own engine noise, Kane could hear other motorcycles behind him.

It took less than twenty minutes to reach the hotel where Kane's other Harley sat. Hunter screeched to a halt. Sam literally jumped from the back of the bike and made time across onto the other one. He started it fast and revved the throttle.

"Come on! Let's go! If you have anything else here, forget it. They are right on our tail!" Kane yelled at them, turning at the same time to look back up the road. "Like I said, 'Willowy', if you need to use the gun... do... with my blessing." He noted she was shaking and that wasn't good. "Get off the bike. Go with Sam. Now, do it...!"

"Kane... no..." she screamed at him.

"Do it... you want to get us all killed? Hunter and I will distract them. Give me my gun and the other one... hurry... and then go..." He virtually pushed her from the Harley.

'Willowy' did as she was asked, handed him both guns and ran to Sam. She jumped on the back of Sam's Harley.

"Dad, I can help you..." Sam blurted out without even thinking.

"*Dad...*? He's your father? Seriously?" 'Willowy' scrambled up behind him and stared back at Kane.

"Yeah, he is... now do what he tells you and hang on to me. I ride as fast as he does..."

"But you just can't leave him..." she was freaking out. She had only just met him and now she was losing him.

"Lady, you may have slept with him, but you sure don't know him. He and Hunter will take care of them while we get the police. At least they will hold them off."

"How the hell can they hold them off? And how did you know I slept with him? We just shared the room!" Was she that transparent?

"Sure you did. I know my father and he doesn't just sleep in a room with a woman… now, hold on to me while we get the hell out of here!" And he turned the bike away from Kane and made great haste out of the parking lot and down the road.

'Willowy' took one last look and Kane at her, and she and Sam disappeared in a cloud of dust. She had the feeling that she would never see him again and tears rolled down her cheeks and onto the back of his son.

Chapter 31

"**O**ver there," yelled Kane. "See them? Boise and about ten other bikers coming down the highway." Kane turned the Harley just slightly to face full on the charging Jon Hordes.

"I see them. He thinks you took his extra pay from him. Why don't you just pay him off? You have the money," stated Hunter.

"What? Pay him off? Are you crazy… kill the son-of-a-bitch maybe? But pay him off?" Kane looked at Hunter like he was nuts.

"Just a thought… you have both guns?" Hunter was looking at Kane.

"Yeah, I do… the girl could not have done it… You think we should stand and fight or go?" Kane was ready to turn the engine off on the Harley, and then he thought better of it. This was a hotel. He looked at it. Not a huge place, but still one where civilians were and he was a cop, one who was supposed to know better than to hold gun-fights in the parking lot. There were other people there, and one of two of them had stepped outside the place to see what the noise was about, and then had run back inside to either call the police or hide. Kane heard the main lobby door bang shut behind them. No where to hide there. Why not take the fight to the Angels? That was it.

"Cover me!" and Kane rode the Harley slowly out onto the road avoiding cars that weaved around him, horns blasting at him.

"What?" yelled Hunter, still astride his motorcycle, a look of total disbelief on his face. "Kane, don't be so crazy… we all know you have a death wish, but god almighty, don't do it… you have kids back home!"

"Yeah, I do… and here, too…" his voice trailed off as he rode away, the engine noise almost drowning out his words.

"What? What did you say?" Hunter was astounded at the comment. What the hell did Kane mean? Sam had left.

Kane could not hear him now. All he was aware of was the adrenalin rushing in his ears, and the power he now controlled. He stopped the Harley right in the middle of the highway, engine purring in the warm sun, his hands reached for both guns.

He was a formidable-looking foe. His jacket stretched across his chest. In each hand he held a .357 and on his face he wore a look of sheer determination. The trees on the side on the highway gave the bikers some cover. For Kane, there was none!

"Kane..." yelled Hunter. "God damn him!" and he left his Harley where it stood. Pulling his gun out of his own jeans he took off after his boss. "He's gonna get us both killed... Kane..." he yelled, but Kane could not hear, nor did he want to.

"Son-of-a-bitch, who the fuck does he think he is? He is gonna take us all on... doesn't he know what fear is?" Boise sat astride the bike and waited for Kane. "You blokes... the bounty hunter is mine. His partner is all yours..." he didn't finish his statement.

"Boise," Kane yelled at the top of his lungs. "This isn't their fight. Just yours... and mine. You killed the cop, and I screwed you over and shot Jenkins. Your friends are not part of this. Give yourself up!"

"Give myself up?! To whom? To you, a bounty hunter? There isn't any price on my head... yet! No one knows about the cop, except you and Mr. Cheng..." Boise was looking for the other people in Kane's party. "Mr. Cheng left you then, and the girl. Didn't care much for her anyway."

"Maybe you should have cared, Boise. You never know who people really are!" Kane said very smugly.

"Is that right? Jenkins died, Kane... right after you left. What do you think about that? Thing I can't figure is why he wanted you stopped. He did, you know. I was supposed to keep you there till he got to the ranch. He didn't want you reaching Alice Springs or anywhere near there for some reason... You know why, Kane?"

"Yeah, I know why... now... best if you don't though..." Kane's voice was lower.

"And how do you suggest I don't find out… from you? You will talk. There are only two of you!" Boise glanced behind him. "Ten of us… if I don't get you, they will! Then you will tell me exactly what is going down here… right?"

"No, not right…" and Kane aimed both guns at Boise. "Tell them to back off… all of them, unless you want me to put a bullet in you right where you are!"

Boise laughed at him, out loud, there on the highway in broad daylight, with cars going by, ones that were speeding up to get away from a very obvious violent situation.

Kane fired one shot and hit Boise straight in the kneecap. Boise fell from the bike to the ground screaming in pain and clutching his leg, blood squirting out from the wound like a fissure. "Kill him!" he screamed at his friends.

Kane didn't wait for them to move. Like the professional he was, he fired again, this time hitting another person in the arm. The Angel let go of the bike he was holding on to, and yelled out in pain as he his arm flopped beside his chest. Kane fired again, this time a warning shot, right in front of two bikers who were thinking about pulling their guns. They changed their minds as they saw both Boise and the other Angel dripping blood.

"Anyone else think they can take me? Go ahead, feel free, and take your best shot!" and he all but opened his arms, guns still in his hands.

Hunter came up behind Kane. His gun stretched ahead of him by his arm's length, standing next to his boss. "Don't even think about it, you blokes! I have his back, and in just a few minutes you will hear police sirens coming up the highway. I would suggest that you get the hell out of here and away from that ranch… all except Boise here, and anyone who had a hand in cop killing, accident or not!" Hunter kept the gun on them and Kane sat there, never flinching, ready to shoot anyone that moved.

In the distance police sirens pierced the air. It was all that the Hell's Angels needed to send them packing. One by one they revved their engines, creating dust, and took off back the way they came. The last thing they wanted was a run-in with police. All of them left, except Boise, and his injured friend. Police cars got closer. Silver-gray cars, with bright red flashing lights, tearing up the highway as fast as their engines would let them go.

"Kane... put one gun away... Kane, you hear me?" Hunter offered advice to his boss.

"Yeah, I hear you..." and sticking one gun in the back of his jeans, dismounted, and strode across the road to where Boise lay on the ground, still writhing in pain.

Boise looked up into Kane's face. "You are no fucking bounty hunter. Who the hell are you?"

"Hell would be the right word!" and Kane peered down at him like he was some sort of dirt on the street. "The police will take you and your friend here and find the ranch. Then they will take one of their own away with them that you killed. You will show them the heroin in the shed, Jenkins, wherever you left him, and then they will lock you up. How do I know all this? Because... Jenkins was right. There is another cop in the group... me!" and Kane accidently on purpose kicked Boise's leg as he turned away, causing him to yell out again in pain. "I am your worst nightmare, *Mr.* Boise. Oh, and before I leave you for them to cart away, Mr. Jenkins was not a Mr. nor was he your friend. He is, or should I say was, Ambassador Jenkins and more than likely I will be in trouble for shooting someone with diplomatic immunity. You see, *Mr.* Boise, it doesn't really matter about trouble because it follows me around. I thrive on it. I guess you could say it's my middle name!"

Kane pulled his cigarettes and lighter from his back pocket, slid one out of the packet and put it in his mouth. He flipped his lighter open and lit the cigarette up, replacing the lighter and cigarettes back in his jacket pocket. He took one drag on the smoke. "Cigarette, Mr. Boise? Might be your last for a while. No? Well, don't say I didn't offer." He took another drag, and could see the police cars slowing down, preparing to stop, as others sped on up the highway. "I hear they are playing your tune, so I will leave you." He paused more for effect than anything else. "You said Jenkins was your friend... he ever mention his wife? A woman by the name of Reese Wade? I would think probably not," and Kane happened to glance down again at Boise one last time, and he could see by the look on his face that he knew the name very well!

Chapter 32

"**R**eally! Now isn't that interesting? And how do you know her?" Kane still looked down at Boise. He knew the police were right behind him, but he had to find out before they took the Angel away, or his chance would be lost. He moved his boot closer to Boise's knee, and it loomed… threatening to kick him where it hurt the most.

Behind Kane, Hunter was dealing with cops. Like Kane, he only had ID on him, just a plain driving license, nothing about the AFP. It was always safer that way.

"Can you hold off for a few moments… he is *chatting* to the man on the ground. He has questions for him…" Hunter did his best to stall them.

"Just who are you guys?" and the young policeman, who had left his car, looked across the road to Kane… and he looked again. "Is that who I think it is?" and without waiting for an answer, the young copper took off to see the commander.

"Oh, dear god… he's gonna blow it wide open…" and Hunter rushed across the street after him, but it was too late.

"Commander Branson… that you, sir?" and there the cover was blown as the young policeman came up behind Kane and tapped him on the shoulder. "Very pleased to meet you, sir…" and the cop almost stood to attention.

"Commander Branson? The hot-shot Commander from Sydney? Kane Branson…" and even through his pain, Boise laughed. "Why the hell didn't I connect the dots? You are all she talked about. Some Australian cop she was crazy about. She told her sister all about you the night of the party…"

170 | Janette Anderson

"What party? Sister… what fucking sister?"

"You don't know? She had a sister who was killed in a car crash last year. Her mother and the sister's little girl were in the car with them." Boise stared up into Kane's face. A way out of this mess loomed in front of him.

Suddenly the light came on in Kane's brain. Kane reached down and grabbed Boise by the lapels of his jacket. "What happened to them? Tell me!" he yelled at Boise.

"Why the fuck should I? You are going to send me to jail, *Commander Branson*. No wonder I thought I had a hired gun… I had… your reputation precedes you and then some… tell you what… I will make a deal with you… no jail, and I will tell you anything you want to know. Anything…"

"I can't do that, Boise. You beat a cop to death… one you hoped I would kill for you."

The young cop watched in amazement as they bantered a deal between them. He removed his hat and scratched his short, dark hair, and a look of bewilderment crossed his face. He had heard so much about Branson and now he had met him, and he wasn't sure of the methods of the man in front of him.

"Then you will never know, will you?" His laugh was maniacal. "I guess you know about the family history?" and once more Boise clutched his leg.

That was enough for Kane. "Get him up off the fucking ground, now and into that police car, and then leave us alone. Take a hike for a few minutes, officer."

"Commander, I can't do that…" he looked staggered that the commander would even ask that of him.

"That's an order, young man. Do it, now!" Kane's temper was rising… fast.

"Yes, sir…" and Officer Stone hoisted Boise from the ground and called his partner over to help get him into the police car.

"What did he tell you?" asked Hunter, watching the officers escort Boise to the waiting car.

Kane watched him go, a kind of a look in his eyes, like he would never be at peace. "Reese had a sister, who had a child… and they were in a car with the sister's mother. The sister was killed."

"And you think what? That the child is Leila? If that's so, then how did Reese end up with her as her own? That doesn't make sense." Hunter kicked at the earth beneath his boots.

"Good question… and who was the mother? That's what I need to know and where I can find her… she is the key to all this. She has all the answers. Boise seems to know. I will get the answers from him… one way or another," muttered Kane.

"Kane, you can't beat the shit out of him here… there's a half a dozen cops standing there watching! These are not your hand-picked blokes back at the station… Kane, think about it, please?"

"I already did," and he left Hunter standing in the dust, and headed straight for the police car that contained Boise. He opened the door and sat in the seat next to him.

Hunter believed the least he could do was try to distract the police for Kane, and he sauntered over to them trying to look like he didn't care about Kane and the loud shouting that was now coming from the back of the car.

Officer Stone, all of twenty-two and his partner about the same age, did their best to try to get to the automobile and at least seem to care about the disturbance. "Your boss?" asked Stone, craning his neck at the car

"Yes, my boss. He has his own methods for getting the truth out of people. Generally, they work out okay." Hunter could not resist a smile. He had been that age… once. He changed the subject slightly. "Did you meet up with another Harley down the road? Or did someone radio in?"

"Both… the station got the call and then this blonde-haired Asian gentleman on a Harley flagged us down. Not so much flagged, but ran into us… and the girl with him was going crazy trying to tell us her boyfriend was in trouble up the highway… I assume you are the boyfriend…"

"Actually… no. That would be the Commander! He has that affect on women… they all want to be his 'friends.'" Hunter was being humorous and pointed to where there was a loud slamming of doors, and Kane appeared out of one of them.

The officers watched the man in the leather as he approached them. Hunter was kind of amused by their looks towards Kane.

"Hurt your hand then, boss?" asked Hunter trying not to snigger as he watched Kane shaking his right arm.

"Yeah. Hit it on some wood in the car! Amazing what's in cars lately."

"Find out what you needed to know, sir?"

"Yep. Sister's name is Claudia. Mother is Toni Wade!" Kane said it like it was meant to mean more than it did. He turned towards the officer. "You need us to come to the station with you, officer? Or can you handle this on your own? I do need to give you a statement about someone I shot at the ranch that your fellow officers went racing off to. They will find Ambassador Jenkins there."

Why did that not shock Stone? He was learning all too fast about this hot-shot commander. "You have somewhere else to be, Sir?"

"Yeah, some little town north of here. Alice Springs to find Toni Wade. Apparently she still lives there, and she can answer all the questions I have." Kane was much more confident now.

"Toni Wade, that's the mother... why does that name ring a bell?" Hunter stopped Kane from walking away by lightly touching him on the arm.

Kane glanced at the hand on his arm, but instead of being angry, he smiled. "Maybe cause it's Reese's mother? Or maybe you have heard it somewhere before."

"It seems really familiar for some reason. Maybe, as you say, it's just the Wade bit. You still want company, Kane?"

"Yeah, son, I do," and Kane walked away towards the Harley.

"If you need his statement now, you better be quick... once he rides away, you might not get it till we return," and Hunter went after Kane, with the words still ringing in his ears.

As they walked away, Officer Stone's radio beeped. He answered it and looked up as he heard the call. "Sir, Commander Branson. Stop where you are, please... Reese Wade, she was missing... they found her, sir... she's dead!"

Chapter 33

Kane stopped in his tracks and turned to face the officer. "She's what? Dead? Don't be crazy... we just saw her a few days ago. Is this some sort of joke?"

"No joke, commander... they just radioed me to ask you to call a Mr. Buchanan? You know him, right?"

"Sure. I'll do it right now, because I am sure it's just another ploy to delay me and make me go back to Sydney instead of Alice Springs!" Kane was obviously not happy that, yet again, he was being stopped. He pulled his mobile from his boot.

Officer Stone stared in amazement as the phone emerged from a boot.

"He always keeps it there?"

"Mostly, yes," replied Hunter, not even conscious that Kane did that anymore.

"Not your usual type of commander, is he?"

"Never," and Hunter smiled in a rather amused way at Stone's responses.

Kane walked to his Harley and punched in buttons for Buchanan on his phone. "Yeah it's me. Is Reese dead? I didn't think so. Would be doing the world a favor if she was! No, I don't mean it... maybe! I wonder... ." Kane paused. "She had a sister, Claudia and her mother is Toni Wade. Do me a favor and contact Alice Springs P.D. See if they can trace her. I met a girl named Toni Wade about thirty–eight years ago on my way back from Nam. I stopped off with friends there before going back to Sydney. She was part of a group of exchange students, but she was always in trouble with the law while she was there, so I let the relationship die a natural death. Apparently... she had a child, Claudia, quite possibly mine... and, Buchanan, don't say a fucking word about my morals, or I'll hang up on you!" There was silence that passed between the lines. "Anyway, Boise, the man in custody here, knows the whole damn family, including the Ambassador... the one I just shot and killed," he paused and held the phone away from his ear. A tirade of accusations and abuse hurled its way down the line. Kane listened to some of it... "It was self defense and I have a dozen witnesses. The cops here are going to the ranch where we all spent the night... well, some of us did... speaking of which, where is my son, Sam? Heading back this way? No, stop him! Tell him to put the girl on a flight back to Alice Springs. She's a cop. I don't want to see her again... and tell Sam to go back to Sydney and stay there. No, you may not ask why I don't want to see her. Just do it, if you would. Hunter and I will go on to the Springs... anything else?... keep me posted as to what you find out." He listened to anything that was relevant, then said goodbye and replaced the phone in his boot.

Kane knew they were watching him by the police cars. Sometimes he wished he didn't look like he did. He had to admit he didn't much resemble the Commander of the AFP, anything but, and maybe he should retire, but now it was all he had to live for... that and his children. Last night with 'Willowy' had been pleasant and he needed her, but it was sex, not love, and that's all it would ever be now, but he was a man turning sixty... and he wasn't dead!

Kane walked back to his little group of admirers.

"Is Reese dead?" inquired Hunter, knowing more than likely she wasn't.

"Unfortunately not... I mean no..." Kane replied looking like he wished he hadn't said that out loud. "She is still missing, though. It was another woman they found. Buchanan is taking care of it. Told him to send Sam back to Sydney. He was coming here with the girl..."

"Oh, your girlfriend, Sir..." interrupted Stone.

"She's not... : and he stopped as Hunter was shaking his head side to side. "She's not coming back. She's one of yours from Alice Springs...undercover."

"Really? Very pretty girl! I'll have to look her up some time… you have her name, sir?"

"Yeah, Kane… you have a name for her? And a phone number?" And Hunter dipped his head to hide a smirk that lingered around his mouth and stayed there. "The Commander is good on names and phone numbers… isn't that right, *sir*?"

"Very fucking funny… yes, I have it. Her name is," and Kane hesitated. "Her name is Kelly and I have her cell number somewhere. I'll get it to you."

"You know, Officer Stone… Kelly might take some persuading to go out with you. She likes older men… The Commander here has a special name for her? Right, Kane?" And Hunter smacked Kane on the back, something he never did.

"Enough, Hunter! Don't you have something else to do? And you, also, Officer Stone? Don't you have criminals to catch rather than standing here babbling about some girl?"

Kane again strode towards the Harley, this time hoping to make it without being stopped.

"Did I touch a nerve there with the commander?" asked a bemused Officer Stone.

"Yeah, mate, you did… let's just say… If he gives you the number, don't call her, ok? Might be better for you not to. Better for your career." Hunter followed his boss to the Harleys.

"How old was the girl? Twenty something… geez, what's he got that we don't…" and Stone looked wistfully at Commander Branson. "Maybe I don't want to know…" and his radio beeped again.

Kane swung his leg over the Harley. "What the fuck do you think you were doing there, Hunter?"

"Breaking the tension. You said in front of two cops that you wanted Reese Wade dead. So, I changed the subject for you." He paused, viewing Kane's face, then looked down at the bike and climbed on, revving the throttle as he did. "So, Alice Springs? Or some other unknown destination?"

Kane glared at him as, he, too, was revving the throttle and kicked away the stand. He took off at warp speed, sending dust and road dirt in Hunter's direction. Hunter smiled. He didn't care, only that Kane liked him at last, and it was then that he really envied Sam having Kane for a father. He followed him up the highway, not having a clue to where they were going. He just knew he would follow him anywhere, but he had this feeling deep down that wherever they were headed, Reese Wade would already be there.

On the contrary, Kane knew exactly where they were heading… Alice Springs, and they had little time now to do it in. If Reese had headed there to see her mother and stop her from talking to Kane, they needed to be quick about it. Reese, and more than likely her crooked attorney, would have taken a flight. They had the Harleys. They would need to ride till they dropped to get there. She may not know yet that Jenkins was dead, but she would if she turned on the television, and it would also be in tomorrow's paper. If that didn't tip her off, the police in Alice Springs would. They'd put two and two together, and would be looking for her as next of kin for the Ambassador.

How he, himself, had not been arrested was a miracle. Kane expected for cops to be waiting for him, even though self-defense, he was still wanted for shooting the guy and whether he was commander or not, they would want statements. He had been lucky just not to have been kept for statements. Hunter was right. He changed the subject nicely for him. He wasn't thinking when he said that about Reese Wade, and Hunter had been.

Now, he needed to concentrate on riding. His mobile was in his boot and if he felt it vibrate he would stop. The only call he wanted was from Buchanan, with an address. Buchanan still had sources to find this woman. Kane wondered if he would recognize her. Thirty-eight years had gone by. All he remembered was the whole group. Most of them were blondes with great shapes. That was then. He had to admit Leila was a nice little girl and he felt sorry for her, being shoved from one person to another.

So intent was he in his thoughts and the sound of two Harleys, he didn't notice how far they had ridden. Soon it would be dark, and they hadn't stopped for hours. They still had around four hundred miles to go. Kane realized how tired he was, and that Hunter was flashing his headlamps at him. Time to stop and take a break. Coming up, Kane could see a rest stop and as he looked down at the nearly empty gas tank. Maybe that's why Hunter was flashing his lights at him. His would be also. Time to pull in… and at least gas up and eat. He slowed from almost a hundred miles an hour to thirty and pulled over towards the rest stop, with Hunter close behind him. As he did, Kane's boot vibrated, and he did something he had never done on his Harley. For one second he lost his concentration and looked ahead of him. There, thundering down the highway right in his path, came a semi. He swerved the bike to miss it and the front wheel caught on a greasy patch of dirt. The Harley slithered across the road and the pathway in a sideward position and it, and Kane, slid some forty feet before it came to a halt. Kane didn't move. He just lay there, on his side in the road, eyes closed, with the Harley's wheels still spinning.

Hunter's bike screamed to a stop at the side of him. He left it with the engine still running… "Kane… Kane," he screamed at the top of his voice. "For god's sake, move! The semi… Kane! It's gonna hit you…"

Chapter 34

"**K**ane! Move… NOW!" and Hunter ran out in front of the semi frantically waving his arms. The driver only swerved because of Hunter and the folks he could see that had run to the end of the rest stop parking-lot to see what the noise was about.

The semi was so close to Kane that the rushing air of the wheels sent dust across Kane's face. He lay there on the hot and dusty road completely unaware that he should be dead by now.

Hunter dropped down beside him. "Don't you dare die on me, you-son-of-a-bitch! You don't leave people who love you!" And there it was said, but it was a love for a father-figure. Hunter's eyes were moist as he turned Kane onto his back till he could see his chest rising. "Kane, wake up!" and Hunter slapped his face just slightly to try to wake him.

By now there were folks all over the place, mostly clamoring to see the man who was almost run down by a semi.

"Could someone get the Harleys out of the road for me?" Hunter said, turning to anyone who would listen.

"Shouldn't we call the police… … ." asked an elderly gentleman with a mobile in his hand ready to dial the number.

"We are the police… maybe an ambulance might be a better idea…" interrupted Hunter, still cradling Kane.

"No ambulance…" whispered Kane. "Get me off the road."

"Kane, you need the hospital… you don't know if you have any broken bones, let alone a concussion… you need to see a doctor." Looking down at him, Hunter tried to make him see sense.

"I don't need any fucking doctor… it just knocked me out. I'll be fine." Kane wasn't sure whom he was convincing, himself, the folks round him, or Hunter. He did know his head hurt and Hunter was probably right.

"This time you are going to do what I say and I think you should visit the hospital…" he didn't finish.

"Sure. Then they can try to kill me there, too…" Kane once more whispered and cut his eyes at his man, glancing round to see who else was watching.

Hunter didn't look surprised that Kane had guessed. "Okay. Let's get you off the road and into the rest stop. I think there is a little café in there. See if they can fix you up…"

"We have to leave here. You know, by now, someone called the police! Come on, get me to the bike. I can ride."

"You can't ride anywhere, mate. If you didn't do damage to you, I think your bike came off worse. I'll get you inside and then take it to the gas station, see what they say about it, okay?" and he helped Kane up, sliding his arm under Kane's arm and round his back.

"Anything to shut you up!" and Kane, with Hunter's help, stood up. "I'm fine, folks," and Kane smiled at their concern and limped to the side of the road, still with Hunter's help and resting very assuredly on him.

"Hurt?" Hunter winced. He knew Kane could take a lot of pain and right now he knew his boss was hurting.

"Like hell! Hoping it's not broken. Get me inside to one of the tables. Take the Harley, see what they say, and if it's bad, leave it. Get them to fix it and we'll get it on the way back. We'll take yours. You drive!"

Now Hunter knew he was in pain. Kane had probably never ridden as a passenger in his entire life. "Whatever you say, *sir*…"

There was a café, with folks there wanting to help him. Hunter and a couple of beefy guys sat Kane in a booth that was way too tight for him. The café was small and probably once was quiet. Now, it was a babbling insanity of folks all wanting to help and tell each other what happened, whether it was right or wrong.

Hunter left him there and took the much dented Harley to the garage. Folks fussed around Kane like bluebottles still insisting they should call the real police, not one who rode a Harley and looked nothing like a cop. It took a lot to convince them not to proceed and let him just rest quietly in the booth.

It was then Kane realized he hadn't looked to see who had called him. He reached very carefully into his boot, and as he did, touched the bone on his ankle. He stifled a yell that did its best to escape from his mouth. Something was broken. A bone, but something not too big, was broken. That couldn't stop him now. He just wouldn't tell Hunter… till they got to Alice Springs.

"God damn it. Doesn't help matters," and he flipped the mobile open and listened to the message. Buchanan had sent him the address of Toni Wade. She had married an American with Australian heritage, but for some reason was still listed under Wade. Two daughters, Claudia, father unknown, and Reese and a son, from the marriage… named Boise! Kane almost dropped the phone. "So, then, Boise, you lied the whole time. Reese is your fucking sister. There was a father from the States, though, that named you Boise…"

But one thing, according to Buchanan, Boise didn't know why the Ambassador wanted Kane detained, nor that he was a cop. The family had very conveniently left that out, and that Kane was Claudia's father and Leila's grandfather. No wonder Boise wanted to cut a deal. Jenkins wasn't his friend, he was his brother-in-law, and Boise wasn't bright enough to figure out Kane's connection to Commander Branson.

Now it made sense. Reese had guessed, quite rightly, that Kane would head to Alice Springs to learn the truth. She knew him well enough to know his moves. Boise had been waiting for him, just that Kane found him by accident instead, and now the semi had been sent to do the work that Boise couldn't finish. Only Kane wasn't dead. Kane sat there thinking. She really had to hate him. Not only had she lost him to Kelly, she had lost him again to another twenty-year-old 'little thing'. That reminded Kane, and he rummaged in his jacket pocket to where the piece of paper lay with 'Willowy's' phone number on it, just in case. He smiled. He had no intention of calling her… nor was he sending it to the cop back down the road.

Kane borrowed a pen lying on the table and wrote down the address Buchanan had left him on his phone. He thought about calling back to Sydney, and then changed his mind. Buchanan would tell him to go home and let the police deal with Reese Wade, and that Kane could not allow. He had to confront her and her mother and find out just why they were doing this now, evening the score by using the child. That just wasn't right. There had to be more to it. He sat there pondering.

"Nice cup of tea, sir… make you feel better."

"What?" asked Kane, totally unaware a young, dark-haired waitress had been watching him.

"Tea or coffee…" She hovered by his table.

"You have some scotch? That would make me feel better. That's if *you* want to make me feel better." He said with emphasis, looking up into her eyes.

"I do… and I have some in the back. They say you're a cop… are you really a cop? You don't look like a cop." As she spoke she chewed gum and popped a bubble before swallowing the gum. She flashed her dark eyes at him.

"I am a cop… commander, actually. And you are a waitress, one who is going to get me a scotch," and he winked at her.

"Maybe… Commander, huh? You ever date, Commander? Like waitresses?"

"Maybe, if they bring me a bottle of scotch." He had elevated the prospects. "And I might leave a big tip, too." He smiled the Branson smile.

"Really, so then I should fetch the scotch." She turned her back to him and wiggled away in her high-heeled shoes to get his bottle of scotch.

No… he wasn't dead… not at all. Now, broken bones or not, he had to get to Alice Springs before someone finished the job. He had to find out why there was so much secrecy.

Chapter 35

Kane downed a couple of scotches in the time it took for Hunter to get an estimate on the bike. He passed by the waitress who was obviously flirting with his boss. Hunter shook his head, and he watched her walk away, her backside in motion.

"Don't you ever quit, Kane?" asked Hunter, as he sat down in the already tight booth.

"Hey, I didn't start it. She did!" Kane replied, downing yet another mouthful of scotch.

"Yeah, but you are old enough to know better. She isn't! Speaking of which… you going to contact the girl you apparently spent the night with?"

"Should I?" Kane looked at Hunter. He was a great looking guy, loyal and devoted to him.

"No. Officer Stone wanted to though," and Hunter fiddled with the paperwork for the Harley knowing that Kane was staring at him.

"Yeah, I know he did, but he doesn't have her number, does he?" and Kane smiled a kind of smug smile. Then the pain in his foot kicked in again and he winced, almost serving him right.

"And you wanted to ride? Right! You can't anyway. Your Harley is a mess. It will take a fair bit of work to put it straight… and money, not that that is a problem for you." He shuffled more paperwork.

Kane heard him and the part about the money, and it wasn't the first time it had cropped up. "Does it bother you that I have money?" He played with the salt and pepper shakers on the table, and as he set them down, they rocked on the uneven table.

"No. Just sometimes, I guess I envy you a little. You have a family, a very nice house and you don't have to worry about what you do and where you go…"

Kane paused. Now was not the time to say it. But he would… very soon.

"You have a good job. You go where you want to, and I know you are not short of money… I pay too well for that to be the case!" Kane picked up the menu and scanned it very half-heartedly.

"Yeah, you do, boss. I can't deny that and so does the AFP, when I am there, that is…" and Hunter laughed, but still there was sadness in his voice.

Kane changed the subject. "We should grab some food and go. We can still make Alice Springs before midnight…"

"Please don't tell me you are going to knock on her door at midnight. Are you trying to get arrested, Kane? Why not just find a motel for the night…" Hunter could see that this line of conversation was useless. The expression on his boss's face said it all. "Okay. So we go on tonight. But, yes, let's grab something to eat. My Harley is gassed up and ready to go and I told the mechanic either we, or the AFP, would get yours and pay him. You want to order something fast, I would guess…"

"Very fast. Call my new friend over. She is very fast…" Kane flashed a grin.

"I bet she is…" retorted Hunter.

Kane smiled. They ordered two giant meat sandwiches and a couple more to go with them, some crisps and fruit. While he was eating his, Kane thought about the stuff on his bike. He had just realized it wasn't with him. He waited till Hunter had finished feverishly devouring his sandwich, leaving a big mess of plates and trash on the table.

"Did you get my belongings from the back of the Harley? I would love to change clothes or at least put a damn T shirt on. I feel naked like this," and he looked down at himself. His jeans had grease on them from the accident and his leather was grazed quite badly on the arm. He had been lucky for it not to have been any worse than it was. He felt round his back and his gun was where it should be. His ID rested in his jacket along with his wallet and his pills… there was a thought. A few days without pills. A nice thought.

"Already on with mine… you need them now?" asked Hunter, hoping he really didn't want the T shirt.

"T shirt maybe…"

"I'll get you one. This place must have a rest room in it…" Hunter looked around, and there at the end of the café was a door marked men's room. "Any particular color and which designer T shirt?"

"Very fucking funny! Just get one, and then let's get going. It's already pitch dark," remarked Kane, looking out the rather dirty window. "We gotta go!"

"Okay, okay… I'll go get one for you… be right back," and Hunter rushed out of the door.

"I'll get the check….meet you by the men's room…" That sounded stupid to Kane. "Or around there."

Kane stood up and realized that he could hardly stand on his right leg. He had taken more impact than he thought, and now his arm hurt, as well. He somewhat hobbled to the men's room and after doing what he had to do, proceeded to wash his hands and throw water on his face.

"Ouch!" he looked harder in the mirror. Down the side of his cheek, just above his beard was a large gash. It must have been hidden by his hair while he was seated, and now he had pushed his hair back a little it clearly showed. "Geez. I look like someone beat me up," and he took a napkin from the dispenser and tried to clean his face up. He wondered why Hunter had not told him about it.

The door opened and Hunter entered with Kane's clean black T shirt. "You might have said they are all black… what happened to your face? I've only been gone three minutes!"

"Must have done it when I fell from the Harley… it's fine… really. I'm fine…" Kane stopped speaking for a full minute. "No, Hunter. I am not fine. Not in the slightest." Kane stared back into the mirror. "There is too much going on in my life… I am not sure what to do…" Kane stopped speaking, out of steam.

Hunter was shocked. He had never thought he would hear Kane admit to not knowing what to do. He couldn't think what to say to him, and watched Kane leaning on the washbasin, his thoughts obviously in turmoil.

"You… er… want to talk about it… how about we get the bike and check into a motel. There has to be one round here. I'm thinking you didn't get much sleep last night." 'Oh god, did I say that out loud?' "I mean…"

"I know what you mean and you are right…" and Kane took the T shirt from him. "I could do with a shower…" Kane stopped. "Hunter… thank you for always being there. I know I don't say it much… but thank you, mate." Kane turned to him and suddenly Kane looked beaten down. He took his jacket off and pulled the T shirt over his head, then put his leather back on. "Let's go…" He saw Hunter's look. "Just up the road and find a motel. You have the food?"

"Yeah, I do. Get a few hours sleep and maybe first you should call home… see how Star and the boys are… and Sage. You know she didn't mean it, Sage that is?" He tried to make Kane see sense.

Kane looked away from the mirror directly at Hunter. "She did mean it, and she was right! I do use women. I did it again last night, used her for sex and then said goodbye. Told her I never would see her again, straight to her face. What kind of man does that? And right after I buried my wife, someone I love very much. What the hell is wrong with me, Hunter? I have no moral standard at all. Everyone knows it! It was even a joke at the station. I get praised for it. Is it something one gets praised for?" Kane paused, totally disgusted with himself, but also sad at the same time. He had loved one person more than life and right now he felt he had betrayed her.

"Kane, you didn't betray Kelly, if that's what you are thinking. You had to do what you had to do…" Hunter interjected, his eyes looking straight into Kane's.

"I didn't have to fucking sleep with her last night! I drank too much and smoked some of Boise's weed. I told her to get out and she didn't…"

"Then it's not your fault…"

"Course it's my fault!" and Kane smacked his hands down in the sink in anger, his voice rising fairly loudly. "And I have Sam by some-one else, and apparently a grandchild by the woman we are going to see… Toni Wade… whom I can hardly remember what she even looks like. Is that the way a commander should conduct himself? Is it!? And… god damn it, Hunter, now I have another…"

And the bathroom door opened and they were disturbed by two guys entering the bathroom and Kane's speech stopped very abruptly, as he turned away from them and Hunter.

Chapter 36

It took them only fifteen minutes to find a motel. It was right on the side of the highway and as they rode there on Hunter's cycle, he could feel Kane almost leaning on him, falling asleep. He was wondering what Kane had been going to say when they were interrupted, as Kane had made some strange comments in the last couple days. The motel was very small and was not the best of places, but they only needed to shower and sleep a few hours and then leave. Kane was still insistent on that point. Hunter paid for the room upfront and they parked the Harley as close to the door as humanly possible without taking it in the room with them. And that thought had crossed both their minds.

Kane turned the key in the lock and flipped on the light switch. He could have sworn he saw cockroaches scurrying under the bed. He thought he must be seeing things. He tossed his motorcycle bag on the bed and then decided to look under it. He wasn't seeing things.

"Fucking great. Whose idea was this? We should have kept going like I wanted to do. We have guests under the bed." He sat down on the end of the bed and removed his boots and jacket, putting his mobile into the jacket pocket and thinking he would call home very shortly. "I think we should just shower and go. You first..." and Kane made the mistake of leaning just slightly back on the grubby-looking pillow and within two minutes was fast asleep on the not-so-clean, well-worn cover.

Hunter had been in the bathroom, such as it was. More like a cubicle, but it did sport a shower and the water was warm, even if the floor of the shower wasn't as sparkly clean as it should be. At least the towels appeared fresh and he was glad to change his clothes as well. Donned in new T shirt and black underpants, he emerged into the bedroom still towel drying his long, black hair.

"It's all yours, Kane... left you warmish water..." and Hunter moved across the room to where Kane lay. "Boss, you okay?"

He was breathing very shallowly, and Hunter wondered if Kane was still alive. Then Hunter saw his chest rise just slightly. "Yeah, Kane. You wanted to ride all night. Shower will keep till morning, mate. Maybe, you aren't so tough after all," and Hunter pulled a cover over his boss. He picked up the bag of food and took it to his side of the bedroom and the other twin bed. The bag made a rustling noise as he opened it and Kane stirred just slightly. Hunter decided to eat his half of the food bag before the roaches ate it for him, and he stuffed Kane's half tightly into his cycle bag and zipped it back up, making sure it didn't touch any of his boss's clothes.

Hunter turned out the light and lay back on the covers. He, too, was very tired and he, also, was asleep within a few minutes.

The next thing they both knew was a loud noise from outside and day light streaming through the windows, through very holy curtains that apparently neither man had closed.

"What the fuck was that?" and Kane virtually shot off the bed, pulling the blanket with him, looking down at it like it was his enemy.

"God knows, but I intend to find out..." and Hunter, too, leapt from his bed.

"You might want to put your pants on first, mate..." and it struck Kane's humorous side, as he watched Hunter charging to the door sans underwear.

"What?" and Hunter looked down. "Oh, yeah," and he grabbed his jeans from the back of the chair, zipping himself into them as he went. He didn't bother with boots and still reached the door ahead of Kane.

Opening it, Hunter stepped outside to see almost a fight going on in front of him. He knew the hotel wasn't that great, but this was crazy. Kane moved in behind him and could see what was happening. It didn't bother him too much until they got very near to the Harley. Then it did. He pulled his gun from the back of his jeans, and waited, his arm hanging by his side and his gun hand filled. When the fight took a turn right next to the Harley, Kane pointed the gun at the two young men who were fighting.

"If you don't stop fighting right now, I will shoot one of you fuckers!" he yelled very loudly.

"Yeah, right, old man. What you gonna do about it?" yelled one of the young, longhaired hooligans that was standing there applauding the fight, as he laughed and continued to egg the opponents on.

Kane's face creased in anger.

"Mate… I don't think you should have said that!" Hunter stated, kind of smugly.

The young man laughed again… and Kane fired one shot into the air. The fight stopped instantly and the crowd backed away from both the Harley, and Kane and Hunter.

"You fired at us…" yelled the young fighting man with bloodied knuckles.

"No, not at you… yet! But the next bullet will be at you… so get the fuck out of here. I am in no mood to be awakened by some idiots like you two, and certainly not by a bunch of hooligans at this hour of the morning." He glanced at his watch. Six a.m. "And if you stand there staring much longer, I am going to shoot again… you understand yet? If you think I won't, ask my friend here. He will tell you what a crack shot I am. I never miss what I aim for!"

Hunter thought that was the truest statement Kane had ever made in his life.

Kane turned on his heel and went back into the room, trying not to hobble as he went. Hunter followed and closed the door behind him.

"You want to shower? I will keep watch by the window… just in case. But I think your firing the gun did the trick. When I was that age, it would have scared the shit out of me. *You* would have scared the shit out of me!"

But Kane realized, yet again, what he had done, just like the day in his apartment when he raised his gun to his own neighbor. He had been angry then and now once more had displayed his anger. They were just kids! He had been like that once. His nerves were still on edge, and he needed to calm down before he met Toni. Toni! That was the reason. Normally he was in control, but this time he had no clue what he would be expecting. He wondered what lies Reese had told her, more than likely that she had slept with him, too.

As Kane stood in the shower, with tepid water running down him, tears ran down his face. How he missed his Kelly. How he had loved her and how he had got her killed. She had given him three fantastic children and how he had hoped for more children with her. Then in just a few seconds she was gone... and it was his fault, just like it was his fault that his first wife was dead, raped and murdered while he was drinking. Again, if not for him, she would not have died. And Lilia, Sam's mother, who took a bullet for him. Too many women had suffered protecting him and his lifestyle, and it was time it stopped. Time he grew up, and he smacked his hand against the shower wall, cursing very loudly as he did.

"Kane, you okay in there?" Hunter was just a little concerned. He could hear the water running and he could hear Kane, and he knew that Commander Branson was indeed suffering.

Hunter walked back to his bed and sat down on it. As he did, his mobile phone rang. Hunter flipped it open and answered it. "Mr. Buchanan. Nice to hear from you. The Commander is in the shower and he did plan on calling you back, but he fell asleep. Anyway, we are on our way to Alice Springs, about four hours out. I know he got your messages about the address for Toni Wade. I also know that he is dreading meeting her. Sir," and Hunter paused, "he is having a rough time of it. He is injured and his feelings are catching up to him. I assume you know about the girl from yesterday? Right, of course you do. Did Sam put her on the plane yet? He might want to delay that. Kane does not want to see her again. Maybe keep her there while we are in Alice Springs. Yeah, she's from there. Did you get a report of the accident? Yesterday, a few hours back. A semi tried to stop him from getting to Toni Wade. I am sure that Reese had a hand in it. No... don't send the police to find her. He needs to do it himself. I think he has a broken something in his ankle. But you know Kane..." Hunter paused and listened to Buchanan for a spell. "Sir, Kane keeps wanting to tell me something... you any idea what it is? He seems preoccupied with it? Kane has to tell me? Is he firing me? Is that it...

no, okay... well, I guess I will find out. I'll get him to call you before we leave here," and he closed the phone. Now, Hunter was even more confused. He was sure that Kane was leading up to telling him something and he wasn't so sure he wanted to know.

Chapter 37

Kane emerged from the bathroom clad in fresh jeans, another T shirt and sat down to pull his boots on. He had tied his still wet hair into a ponytail and banded it tight. The gash on his face didn't look as severe as it did last night and it looked cleaner from the shower. He stuffed his gun down the back of his jeans and pulled the T shirt over it.

"Any of that food left?" he asked Hunter.

"It's in your bag… if the roaches didn't eat it. Didn't you see the sandwich when you pulled your clean clothes out?"

"Is that what that was… oops," and he scrambled back to the bag to re-find the food. He pulled a soggy looking sandwich out, opened it and it departed as a missile to the nearest bin. He did, however, find an apple and some crisps, which he devoured in about three bites.

"Anything else to eat?"

"I can go to the vending machines, that's if they have one in tact and not ripped off the wall… you want some soda or something?" Hunter chose his words more than carefully.

"Please… and Hunter, after Alice Springs, you and I have to talk. I… can't deal with it till then… too much else to think about," and Kane looked straight at Hunter almost apologizing to him. "It's just that right now…"

"I understand, Kane… really, I do…" Hunter paused and remembered the call. "I spoke to Buchanan. He called while you were in the shower just to see if you were okay…" 'Another bright statement there, Hunter… dear god, can't you talk to this man without putting your foot in your mouth!' "I'll be back…" and Hunter opened the door to the room and left rather quickly.

Immediately Kane picked up the mobile and dialed Buchanan. "What the fuck did you tell him? Who? Hunter, of course... you didn't tell him, did you? Thank god. I can't explain that right now." Kane paused. He really couldn't. "We are leaving here in about ten minutes. I am sure he told you we only have one Harley now. The other one is somewhat worse for wear now. Yeah. It's a very expensive motorcycle. Can you get the guys to collect it for me just in case we don't come back this way? And don't you ever tell him. That's my place to. Gotta go... call you when we get there," and with that he was gone as the room door opened.

"Got a couple of cherry sodas and some snacks for later... peanuts and chocolate chip cookies," and Hunter threw some to Kane.

Kane was ripping the bag of cookies open as he spoke. "Cherry Sodas? No scotch?"

"You are joking, right?" asked Hunter, somewhat disgusted that Kane would even think of drinking this early and on this day.

"Not really," and he glanced at his watch. It was already gone seven a.m. They were burning daylight and Kane figured that this was a day he might remember for a long time. "Let's go..." and Kane disappeared out of the room and stood waiting by the Harley, impatient to be gone, just like the chocolate cookies were.

Hunter slammed the door behind him and stashed both of their bags on the back of the bike. He climbed on and Kane behind him, and they all but screeched out of the parking lot and left the motel in the dust, quite possibly where it should have been.

Traffic was good as they sped up to Alice Springs. They passed some landmarks on the way and signs that indicated how far they had left to go. They pulled into one stop for the bathrooms and then, this time, Kane sat up front ready to drive. He wanted to go just a little faster than Hunter had. Point was, he had to feel in control, and sitting on the back he wasn't.

They picked up more speed and made better time, and just after noon they approached the outskirts of Alice Springs. As it loomed in front of them, Kane felt his stomach turn over. Even though he had to do this, he was not looking forward to it. He revved the throttle to get more power and sped down the hill towards destiny.

Eventually he slowed down to a mere sixty, observing some sort of speed limit, and then pulled over to the side of the road and stopped the Harley. He pulled the address from his pocket and instead of pulling the piece of paper with that on; he pulled the phone number for 'Willowy' instead. He stopped in his tracks, went to throw it on the road and then thought better of it, returning it to the inside of his jacket.

Hunter watched him and knew that 'Willowy' was not part of the past.

Kane found the other piece of paper and turned slightly to Hunter. "Should not be hard to find. Buchanan gave good instructions how to get there," and he handed Hunter the address.

"Nervous?" Hunter saw Kane's hand shake for one fleeting second.

"Yeah. Silly, huh?" and Kane could feel the engine vibrate between his legs as he started the bike up again.

"Not really. To find out you have another child, and a grandchild all in one go, isn't silly at all." Hunter understood. Trying to convey it to Kane was different.

Kane froze and his eyes darted to Hunter's side. Did he know? Buchanan said he didn't.

"Read them out to me and let's hope the police are not there before we are. You and I know that Reese will be there by now. God knows what she told her mother." Kane paused. He was trying so hard to remember her and he couldn't, all accept what he had been told: but her face, he could not remember at all.

"You can't remember her face, can you?" Hunter asked him, almost afraid of the answer.

Kane shook his head. "There were so many girls and so much alcohol and more…" Had he really said that out loud? Why didn't he just take his own gun out and shoot himself in the foot? Better still, his crotch…

"Go by your instincts… you will know her. You said she was blonde, slim and tall. That's a start. You only go for blondes anyway… right?"

Kane nodded. How wrong was that?

"Okay, well we know she is blonde or was and she is about fifty-six or fifty-seven, right?" He was doing his best to help his boss.

"The group of girls… they were just turned sixteen. Seventeen tops. Exchange students from the US," Kane corrected Hunter.

"So drop a year or two. She still has to be over fifty-four. I guess it depends how she matured and how well she stayed in shape. Didn't you say she was in trouble with the law there?"

"She was. I remember most of them got into drugs…"

"Is that where you learned to distinguish China white?"

"No. That was Nam." Kane wasn't proud of that fact, but it helped him with his career choice. "Okay, let's do this…" and he revved once more and they shot off up the main street towards the directions that Hunter was giving him. They passed some nice homes and some not so nice, and Kane wondered where exactly they were going. Hunter tapped him on the shoulder as he saw the street name.

They stopped at a gate. Kane looked at the number on the building and then looked again at the street sign. There was no way on this earth it was the right place. Hunter climbed off the bike and as Kane parked it, they stood together, both not believing where they were. There had to be some mistake. But Buchanan didn't make mistakes.

St. Joseph of Cluny Convent loomed before them. Large gates and older buildings stood there almost jeering at them, daring them to enter to find the truth.

Kane pulled his mobile out of his boot and dialed. "Yeah, Buchanan? Where the hell have you sent us? We are at some convent on the outskirts of Alice Springs. This can't be right. Some relative with the same name die there and you got the names mixed up?" Then there was silence. "She's a nun? How the fucking hell can she be a nun? She had three children… and a husband…" More silence as Kane listened. "And you knew this from when? Yesterday, and you let me continue on up here? I had to find out for myself? Well, I found out! Go in? Why? Who else is there? Reese? That figures! Okay, as we are here, we will go. By the way, is the girl still down there? Okay, you can put her on the plane now. Send her home." Kane hung up the phone. "Well, Reese beat us here, which is no surprise… so let's meet the grandmother of my grandchild…"

Chapter 37

Kane opened the large iron gates with some hesitation. They passed through the gardens that seemingly were very unkempt for Alice Springs. Statues stood on each side of them as they walked a long path to the door. The place itself looked a little deserted, with the windows closed, and the main door shut tighter than hell. Kane looked for a bell. There wasn't one, so he banged on the oak door as hard as he could. Still nothing.

Kane pulled his mobile out again. This time it was seeking refuge in his pocket. He dialed Buchanan yet again. "We are outside the door and there is no one here! What explanation do you have this time? The place is empty… looks like anyway… you sure this is the right place? The only sign of nun's being here are gravestones." Kane looked around as he spoke. That's pretty much all he could see, gravestones and large trees that looked like they needed water. "We will look round the back, but this almost looks like a setup… do you know where Leila is and, better yet, where is that creep of an attorney, Davis? She is with the police… okay, but where is he?..." and as he spoke, a shot rang out and missed him by inches burying itself in a nearby tree. "We found him… gotta go… shots fired… send back up!" and Kane was gone, pushing the cell into any pocket that was close.

"Which way?" and he pulled his gun, as he yelled to Hunter.

Hunter pointed to the side of the building where several old gravestones sat. There was plenty of cover for a sniper to be hiding. But why only one shot, why not more? Did that mean a lone gunman or was it just a warning? He pointed a route for Hunter to take, around the side and coming out the back of the building behind the shooter. Hunter nodded that he understood and took off with gun raised ready to fire.

Kane positioned himself behind the arch of the doorway, hiding most of his body, but leaving just enough for the sniper to still be able to pinpoint him. Suddenly, out of nowhere, there was another shot, this time from the opposite side of the church. It hit the doorway and the bullet embedded itself in the wood next to his head. That was too close for Kane. He had to move, and now, before they killed him. Whomever they were, they were good. And Kane had an idea who one of them was, if not both. He waited till he thought Hunter was in a good position, and then Kane stepped slightly to his left and fired a shot towards the area the second shot had come from. He fired again, this time quite obviously hitting more than a tree. There was a shriek, a man's shriek, and the sound of bushes parting in the person's wake. Then it was quiet. He had wounded someone, but, somehow it wasn't the right someone. Kane went to take a step and his ankle all but gave away. He winced, but he didn't cry out. What he did do was give his exact position away, and this time, as the shot rang out, Kane dropped to the ground.

From where Hunter was positioned he could see Kane and he saw him drop to the floor. He thought he had been shot and he rushed out of his hiding spot, straight into the next bullet. He dropped like a brick as the bullet hit him in the upper-chest sending his gun flying from his hand and blood spurting onto his clothes. His T shirt was soaked in seconds and, as he lay there, he thought he was going to die.

"Hunter," yelled Kane. "Hunter... I see you, hold on. I'm coming!" and Kane attempted to get across the distance between them. As he did, another shot rang out, this time at him. He ducked, and now he was counting bullets. At the most, the person had two left maybe three, depending what size .357 they were using, and if it was whom he thought was behind the trigger, they would only have two left.

Another shot rang out as the person seemed to panic just slightly. Realizing the fact they were almost empty, the person turned to run. All Kane could see was black leather pants and jacket. The black helmet hid the whole head and face. He wanted to go after them, but he had to see to Hunter, make sure he was still alive.

Kane dropped to the ground next to Hunter. Blood was gushing from the wound. He put his hands on him to stem the flow of blood, pushing hard trying to see just how bad it was.

Hunter was still conscious. "Go, boss. Go get them! It's all up to you now! You know who it is… get them… for your wife." His breathing was labored.

And Kane left him… left Hunter on the ground possibly dying. But he was right; this was a way to even it out for his Kelly.

Kane could hear a motorcycle's engine revving and then speeding off. He ran to the Harley, shoved the gun down the back of his jeans, jumped on and, with great haste, started the engine. Dirt and dust flew behind the wheels as he took off after the shooter.

They both blazed trails of dust and speed as one followed the other. Hunter's Harley was faster than the other bike and Kane gained on the smaller motorcycle. Kane pulled alongside the other bike sending traffic on the highway into total chaos. He tried to make the other cycle slow down by forcing it into the brush alongside the road. But still they kept going, weaving and dodging through the oncoming traffic, Kane much more experienced at riding on this side of the street. In the distance he could hear police sirens and as he looked up into the afternoon sun, several police cars were coming over the hill towards them. There was almost a glare of lights and sun combined as one and it was then as his Harley tried one more time to force the motorcycle into the brush. The police cars came to a halt, forming a barrier to stop the motorcycles going any further, a formidable sight.

Kane instinctively slowed down. He could see the police positioning themselves, guns in hands ready to fire… not at him… but at the rider next to him. He couldn't let them die like that… why didn't they stop… why… and it was then he yelled out loud.

The rider could not hear him through the helmet and even if they could, they would not have stopped. Everything was lost, especially the thing they wanted the most. They had tried to kill him and had failed, just like they had failed all along to keep him.

Kane screamed at the cops ahead of him not to open fire, not to shoot… but it was too late. He watched in slow motion as he swerved his Harley to the right and away from the other bike. Suddenly, he

202 | Janette Anderson

didn't want to die. He slowed to a crawl as he watched the hail of bullets hit the rider. There was no way they could survive that. The bike fell and lay sprawled with shredded tires spinning, the person lying still in the grime, a small pool of blood running out onto the dusty road.

Kane dropped the Harley and ran to the body lying there. He looked down as the person lay still and in the background he could hear cops running to them both. He bent down, on one knee, and gently removed the helmet that hid the identity.

Kane flinched. It hit him hard.

"You! Put your hands in the air! Do it now!" screamed the uniformed cop right behind him, gun pointing at Kane's head. "Do it! Now!"

Kane did as he was asked. He raised his arms high and the cop grabbed Kane's gun from the back of his jeans. "Down on the road. Face down. Now!"

Again, Kane did as the overzealous cop asked of him. He couldn't blame the cop. At his age, he would have been the same. He lay there, his face turned towards Reese Wade. She was dead on impact… a dozen bullet holes in her. Her hair flopped out of the helmet when he had raised it. Long eyelashes that once fluttered at him lay still now. He could have saved her; he had tried, knowing full well it was her. But she had hated him too much to stop loving him, and she paid for it with her life.

"Back pocket of my jeans… my ID. Call it in to Sydney headquarters. They will tell you who I am. Ask for Dan Lord or Buchanan."

"Any reason we should?" asked the rather over-confident officer.

"If you want to keep your job, I would do it…" replied a very subdued Kane.

"Call it," the officer yelled to his partner. "Give them a description of this biker here, and get the ambulance here as fast as possible. One person down."

Kane heard the junior officer making the call and he heard his tone change instantly. The young man whispered to this partner.

"Commander Branson, I am so sorry. We were just told to stop everyone one way or another…" and the partner was red from embarrassment. He had the commander of the AFP lying face down on the concrete like some convict, and figured his chances of promotions had just gone out of the window.

Kane rose up from the ground, snatched his gun back from the officer and turned back to the body of Reese Wade without saying a word to him.

"Why? Why did you have to end it like this? So many questions unanswered. Who were you protecting there at the convent? Your mother? Is she alive or dead?" And Kane's head fell forward, and he shook it from side to side. "Officer, you treat her with respect, not like some piece of meat to haul away. Get any ID on her and get it to me. Get one of your officers to drive me back to the convent. My bodyguard is there... and I need to see him."

He pulled his mobile out of his jacket and dialed Hunter's number. There was no answer ... and Kane feared the worst.

Chapter 38

Kane sat in the police car with sirens blaring as they sped back up the highway to the convent. The Harley was evidence in a crime scene. He kept trying Hunter's number... nothing.

"Dear god, he cannot die... not now!" Just then his mobile rang. "Yeah, Hunter? Oh, it's you... what the fuck did you tell those cops to do? They killed her, Buchanan. Shot her down like some dog in the street... I know she tried to kill me... and her attorney, right? The police have him? Where is he now? One thing you all did do right, then! But for her to die in a hail of bullets just doesn't seem to be right. Now the child doesn't have a mother of any description... and the father... where is he? No one knows? What do you mean? The kid only has a grandmother now... yeah, and me! Right now, all I am interested in is Hunter... did they find him?" Kane was almost frightened to ask. "Is he okay? He doesn't answer his mobile... at the hospital? Which one, where? On my way. And Buchanan where is Toni Wade... she's with him? How the fuck can she be with him? She found him?" and Kane hung up the phone. He thumped the side of the car with his fist. "Officer, where is the nearest hospital from the convent?" he didn't wait for the reply. "Just take me there and hurry. Can't you go any faster? I'll take responsibility for anything that happens... just drive, man!"

The driver picked up speed and the officer with him nodded his head that it was okay to do this. They passed the convent and Kane could still see police at the scene. Lights were flashing and the whole place looked like a war zone instead of the peaceful place he had just left not half an hour ago.

Kane sat in the back, his arms resting on the leather seats and his eyes wide staring through the front windows between the officer's shoulders. "How much further can this place be?" As he said the words, he looked up. There in front of him loomed Alice Springs Hospital. It wasn't as big as the ones in Sydney, but big enough. The police car pulled into one of the spaces by the emergency door and Kane almost fell out of the car to get in there. The cop riding shotgun followed him in to give Commander Branson clearance to Hunter.

Kane rushed inside the building and up to the nurse's counter. "Looking for Hunter McLeod, brought in by police. He has a gunshot wound in his chest," he said, breathing hard.

The nurse didn't hurry, just glanced up at him. She flipped through paperwork. "Relative?" she asked him.

"What?" asked Kane, a look of amazement on his face.

"Is he a relative? Only relatives can go in there. Doctors are with him. You need to wait outside..." and she carried on with her paperwork, totally disinterested in anything else.

Kane went to answer her.

It was then the officer took control. "Nurse, this is Commander Branson of the AFP. He needs to know how his bodyguard is. We know he is in with doctors, but we also need to know his condition. Please find out for the commander... now!" and the look of quiet authority was there.

The nurse's attitude changed. "Right away, Commander Branson." She flipped much faster through the papers. "He is critical. Again, sir, relatives only allowed in there." This time her voice was lower and more controlled.

This time Kane answered her almost forcing the words out. "Look, lady! He's my son!"

"Oh, in that case you can go in and talk to the doctors. Door on the left," and she pointed to the door.

"Sir, I can get you in. You don't have to say anything just to get past the door..." the officer volunteered as he removed his police hat.

"Right... I know, but it helped..." The look on Kane's face was ice cold and totally unreadable.

The officer did not know if Kane was telling the truth or not, but it had got them past the reception desk and down to the ER room. This officer was older and wiser and had learned when to ask and when not to. The officer thought about asking Kane if it was the truth, but decided against it, as judging by the commander's face, he was in no mood to be questioned. They stopped at the door and a male nurse came out to see the police.

"You a relative, sir," the male nurse asked.

There was that question again. This time he didn't answer. He just nodded.

"Perhaps then you can give me more information on him," the nurse asked, with a formal looking clipboard and paperwork in hand.

"What do you need?" asked Kane rather reluctantly.

"Age, parent's info, any medical history we should know and allergies to medication. Things like that." The nurse opened the paperwork ready to take notes.

"First… before anything else… is he going to make it?" Kane didn't just ask, he demanded to know.

The nurse could see a small amount of blood on Kane's jacket sleeve where he had held pressure on Hunter's chest. "You okay, sir? I see blood on you."

Kane looked at his wrist. The jacket did have blood on it and his jacket was torn from his own accident. "I'm fine… how is he?" Kane said in a slightly louder voice.

The nurse, in his starched white shirt and pants, replied. "He is in critical condition, and badly needs a blood transfusion… we are, right now, looking at his blood type." As he spoke the door opened and a lab technician stepped out into the lobby with the results.

"AB positive, sir" and the technician disappeared to where he came from.

Kane froze, turning ashen as he did. If he had any doubt before… now he didn't. "That's my type! I will donate blood for him. Can I see him?"

"You sure you are alright, sir…" he thought the man in front of him was about to pass out.

Kane reached inside his leather and pulled the pills out. Popping one into his mouth, he again came back to reality. He breathed very deeply and leaned on the shinny, white hospital-wall for a second.

The officer leapt into action. He put his hand on Kane's shoulder. "Commander, you feeling alright, sir?" he knew what kind of pills those were.

The nurse raised his eyebrows. He thought he had seen this gentleman before. He did read, and had seen the pictures of Kane on the front of last year's Police Gazette issues. "Commander Branson, would you like to sit a minute, sir?"

"No, I would not like to sit! I would like to see my son!" Now Kane was agitated and it showed. He was with strangers and he didn't like that, and he didn't like being side tracked.   He stood up straight again and, as he did, his head turned slightly… and Kane thought he had died and was in heaven. Leaning against the opposite wall stood a woman dressed head to toe in white, with the sun streaming from the big bay windows making her look like an angel. All down the front of her was the color red and her habit was covered in blood. Most likely Hunter's blood. "Toni," and he whispered so low that he hardly heard the name himself. He was amazed he recognized her, but he had, after all this time.

She didn't look her age. In his eyes she still looked sixteen, and she stepped forward as he caught site of her.

Her voice was soft. "Kane. You have hardly changed. Even your hair is as long."

He stared at her and it all came flashing back to him like it was just yesterday… in her high heels and short skirts. "Toni… I… er ," and he looked down at her robe. "Thank you for finding Hunter. I need to see him… make sure he is alive and give blood. Stay with the officer here till I come out?"

"Of course. I have to give statements to the police. I haven't done that yet. I saw everything, Kane. I saw my daughter try to kill you…" and she looked down, ashamed of her own family. "I know what she did with Leila. I will tell you everything. So much to tell you with so many years gone by."

"I am so sorry about Reese. I tried to stop the police firing..." He stopped speaking... too many emotions all welling up at the same time. "And Claudia, it was Claudia, right... she was my daughter? And Leila is my grandchild?" Kane wasn't even sure he had it all right. His eyes were those of a tired man.

Toni Wade nodded.

"Commander... we should go to Hunter. He needs your blood or there is a chance he won't make it." The nurse needed him to go, and now. There wasn't much time left.

"I have to go. I'll be back. I have to try to make amends to you..." Kane was a lost man, right now, more than he had ever been in his life....

Toni reached forward and touched his arm very gently. "I will be here. Go to your son, Kane. He needs you." And she turned away from him. "As I did once!"

Chapter 39

Most hospitals had a chapel and this one was no different. Toni sat in there and waited for Kane. At the end of the wooden pew stood a police officer… after all, Toni was a key witness and possibly an accessory to the crimes committed. Certainly her statements were needed and she seemed to be the only one who knew the whole story. She thought about Kane and what he must be going through now.

They let him into the ER and he lay on a bed near Hunter. He wasn't given time to actually see him properly. Kane did turn his head towards Hunter, and could see all kinds of apparatus attached to him. He turned a little further and could see the monitor with his heart rate. Kane shuddered, reminding him of his own time in the hospital. It was all too real for him. All around him was clinical white walls and sterile floors. Here lay a man with a bullet in him that didn't know he had a father, a father that had known for several months he had another son. Kane's mind drifted as they took more blood than they needed… just in case.

It had been Buchanan who had made the discovery, quite by chance. When Sam Cheng had proved to be Kane's eldest, someone else had shown up on the radar. Buchanan, once more, had investigated and found that Hunter McLeod was an orphan, so it seemed, and had entered the AFP as a career to set himself up for life. He had succeeded, but had done too well and brought attention to himself. To advance further, a thorough background check had been done, before he could become Kane's bodyguard. It was then Buchanan found out Hunter was the son of someone in the AFP. He had taken several months longer to discover for a fact that he was Kane's son. It was proved without doubt while Kane was in Japan and Hunter had been sent out there, just in case. Buchanan and Kane had kept the secret and Kane was going to tell Kelly when they got back home from Iraq. The chance to tell her never came.

When Hunter said his boss had six children he was right. He did have six... now. Before that, he had seven. Kane now had the task of telling Hunter just who he was and he wasn't quite sure how Hunter would take it, and more than that, how the rest of the children would accept him, especially Sam. The two were just months apart from each other. They were his main concern.

"Commander... Commander Branson... we have enough blood. Would you like something to drink? Orange juice and a biscuit... or maybe some chocolate?" The over- diligent nurse was back at his side in his crisp white shirt and pants, making Kane wonder if he ever got dirty. He made Kane bend his arm and then produced a Band-Aid that he popped on Kane's arm where there now seemed to be a gaping hole from the needle's insertion.

"Scotch would be nice... can you arrange that for me?" and Kane winked at him.

"No can do, sir... would you like to sit up a little?" and the nurse propped a pillow under Kane's head. "Not too fast... we don't want you blacking out on us..."

"How's my son?" he asked, much more serious.

"Still in bad shape. Bullet has to come out, and he has lost a lot of blood. But he's very tough, which I'm sure you know. Are you aware of any medications he has an allergy too?"

"I am sorry, but I don't..."

"Any health problems or history of them? Things we should know?"

Kane shook his head side to side. He hadn't a clue other than those listed in his dossier. "I'm sorry, I can't help you... I don't even know who his mother is..." He said it out loud, the thing he didn't want to admit. He knew that Hunter didn't know either. Apparently Hunter had tried to find her and couldn't. What a great admission for a Commander to make. Maybe he should resign on moral issues.

"That's ok, sir. We often have cases like this one..." and the nurse wrote something on the clipboard.

"Of course you do. Every day! I'll take the orange juice now, please," and Kane sat up, swinging his legs over the side of the bed. He looked around for his leather jacket and T shirt. "Can I get closer to him?"

The nurse looked like he wanted to say no, but the commander had rank on his side and he figured Kane would use it if he had to. He didn't look like a man one would say no to.

"Just for a moment. We need to get your blood in him," and he helped Kane off the bed.

"Hasn't done him much good lately, has it?" Kane quipped. That's how he felt.

The nurse caught the innuendo. He handed Kane his T shirt and Kane slipped it on over his head. He was kind of tired at everyone staring at the scar on his chest; in fact, he was kind of tired of people staring at him, period.

"Put this on also…" and the nurse handed Kane a mask. "Just in case…"

Kane took it from him and slipped it on. He moved as close as he could to Hunter, without getting in the doctor's way. He looked down at the man lying there. One who would give his life for his boss. Kane felt he had judged him too harshly in the past and perhaps when he was well, he could make it up to him. He whispered very softly. "I love you, son." He took a step back and watched Hunter's chest rise very slightly as blood seemed to gush from the hole in his chest. "Dear god… how can he survive?"

"Apparently the same way you did, sir," and the nurse moved him out of the way. "Like father, like son!" and he ushered Kane outside to the waiting area. "Wait here. As soon as they know something, I will get you, okay?"

"Yes…" and Kane sat down on one of the well-worn benches in the waiting-room. He slid his leather on. For some reason, he was cold now, and he nursed the orange juice he had been given. Now he wished he had taken the chocolate offered as well. There were police everywhere he looked. He wondered where Toni had gone and came to the conclusion she was either giving statements or was more than likely in the chapel.

The older officer from the police car stepped up. "You need anything, Commander?"

"Yeah," and Kane raised tired eyes up to him. "Some chocolate and coffee. And some information."

"Of course. I'll get that for you, and the information? If it's the nun who found your son, she's in the chapel. Straight down the lobby and on the right. You want me to go and get her?" the cop asked, just trying to help his boss.

"I'll go in a minute. Just need some time, and some chocolate in me. Got to make a couple of calls back to Sydney. Need to check up on my other kids."

"How many do you have, commander?" asked the cop innocently.

"Six… was seven… now six… better not be five," and he looked towards the operating theatre door. That was said with a threat.

"I'll get your drink and chocolate, sir" and the officer was gone, just a little bit afraid of the commissioner and the trouble that might be following him around.

Kane stood up, moved to the entrance of ER, and pulled his mobile out to make calls.

The first one was to Sam on his private mobile. He didn't answer. Kane had wanted to talk to him the most, but it didn't seem like that was going to happen. He needed to tell him before anyone else that he had a brother. He hung up the line and called Buchanan instead.

"Yeah, me… he is still critical. I had to tell them here he was my son. Blood type is the same… rare. Yeah, of course I gave him blood. Why the fuck wouldn't I? He is my son. I tried to call Sam to talk to him. Airport? Oh, right… the girl? Oh, Sita and the baby… they have arrived… maybe better to wait till I get back to tell them all together. You didn't say anything did you? Thank god! It all needs to come from me. Changing the subject… did they get the fucker who tried to run me down in the semi? Good! And they have the lawyer… Toni, yes, she is here. I did recognize her. She said she knows everything, so I guess I will go and talk to her and then let the police here deal with it. I have to talk with her though, but I am guessing they will arrest her. I can put in a good word for her, see that she gets an easy ride.

Am I okay?" Kane paused. He had known Buchanan too long to lie. "No. I am not. I am ashamed of myself, Buchanan. Things are going to change when I get back. And, I am tired. I should take a vacation soon. Get away with the younger kids... my heart... it's fine, just a little frayed round the edges. Pumps a little slower nowadays... Buchanan... did Sam put her on the plane for here? 'Willowy'? Good. Hopefully I will be out of here. As soon as we can, fly Hunter back to a Sydney hospital... he has to get the best treatment possible. Because he's my son? No. Because he stopped a bullet for me!"

Suddenly, out of nowhere, bellowed a sound that Kane was very familiar with. "Code Blue." Hunter was flat lining. Kane could only stand and watch as everyone nearby tried to save his son.

"Don't you die. Don't you die you son-of-bitch! You have to know you have a father!"

Chapter 40

Toni could hear the "Code Blue" from the chapel. She clutched the cross in her hands. Usually it hung round her neck. She didn't want to be responsible for another of Kane's children's deaths. There was enough blood on her hands already.

The officer asked her to sit down and give her statement. He figured that was as good a place as any for a nun to confess. He called a female officer into the side room of the chapel and he put a large notepad on the table and waited for her to start. He clicked the pen a couple of times in the hopes she would just open up and let go. She did.

"My name is Toni Wade. I am originally from Boise, Idaho and was a U S exchange student with a girl from Alice Springs almost, I guess, forty years ago. I wasn't the brightest girl in the class, and not the most honest. While I was here, I met a group of soldiers on their way back from Nam... a mixed bunch, from different parts of Australia. Not quite sure why they stopped here," and she tried to remember why. She couldn't. "Anyway, they did. Amongst them was a young, but very tough guy named Kane Branson. One night, there was a huge party and he was one of the soldiers there. It was full of guys and I made a bet with some of the girls that I could sleep with the four best looking ones there. We were all pretty drunk, and some of the girls were doing drugs. The girls called me out on the bet. By that time, I was totally drunk and Kane was one of the guys I had sex with. He was the best looking of them all and I fulfilled the debt and worked my way into their crowd..." She paused, remembering... a shy smile crossing her face.

"The men left after a couple of weeks. I saw Kane again, maybe a couple of times, but the dates didn't go so well, and he obviously didn't remember ever having slept with me. He was eager to go home and he did. I never saw him or any of the guys again, except one of them, Tom Turner. He was the only vet that stayed behind. He didn't seem to be like the rest of them, quiet and reserved, except when he drank, which became more and more frequent, and he was an American with Australian parentage. He had stopped there because he had served with Kane's unit and also to see his relatives before he left for the States. We started dating and were married within three months." Again, she stopped.

It was quite obvious to the officer that they were painful memories. He wanted her to go on, but he didn't want to rush her. She had to tell this in her own time.

She glanced around the room. It was bare compared to the chapel with its ornate statues of angels and old redwood pews. She continued. "The wedding was fast, for the main reason that I was pregnant. I had no idea which man was the father. Nor did I really care right then. It could have been anyone of the four. I had the baby as I turned seventeen. She was gorgeous. Blonde hair and bright blue eyes, and then I knew who the father was, and, so did Tom."

"Commander Branson ..." the officer interjected without thinking. He was caught up in her story.

"Yes, Commander Kane Branson. Even though she had his coloring, I wasn't one hundred percent sure. I thought her hair color might change, you know, grow darker, but it didn't. Tom was a good man and accepted Claudia as his own. Not much else he could do, really. He wanted us to move, though, back to the States, just in case. He didn't want Kane claiming the child; and it was okay for a while. Reese followed fast on Claudia's heels and then came a son, Boise. Reese and Boise were both dark-haired, like their father, and he adored them and they him. Both turned to their father and Claudia to me. The children were worlds apart. Claudia, a roamer, looking for excitement... and Reese a bookworm and an A plus student. Boise was a born biker, even as a little boy. Tom taught him how to fight and how to kill. They would go hunting all the time. But back to Claudia... she stayed a blonde, and as she grew up she looked more like Kane than ever, sporting striking good looks and with those captivating blue eyes."

The officer wondered if she was talking about her daughter or Kane.

"Tom started drinking with much more frequency and he became violent. The police came several times and we tried counseling. Nothing worked. We divorced when Claudia was ten, and he won custody of Reese and Boise, and I of Claudia. I think deep down Claudia was the problem for him. Tom stayed in the States and the two youngest stayed with him. Claudia and I came back to Alice Springs. I had friends here who gave me a job and vouched for me working here. At first, I wanted to seek Kane out and tell him he had a daughter. I fully intended to do that when one day I was reading the paper and there was his picture... up and coming officer in the Australian Federal Police, married with a child. He had medals on his chest. I knew I could not do it. Not interrupt his life. So we stayed here and I worked, and Claudia grew up. She came home one day and said she was pregnant... she like me, had no clue whom the father was. Claudia was a popular girl and she dated a lot. So we dealt with it and we raised the child between us. It worked out well. Kane didn't know he was a grandfather, and Claudia never asked whom her real father was." She stopped.

The officer felt sorry for her. She had made mistakes and now she was paying for them over and over again.

"May I have some water?" asked Toni.

"Of course," and he sent the female officer in search of liquid refreshments. She was back in five minutes.

"Thank you," and Toni drank it down in one go. "All was fine until Boise decided to come back to Australia. He had become a hardened biker and he set up a gang over here. That wasn't so bad until Reese came to visit. She had changed from the young girl I knew. She was a US Marshall and all she talked about was an Australian Federal Agent she had met. She told me and she told Claudia. She would always look at Leila kind of strange, like somehow she recognized her. Reese was obsessed with the guy. Much older than her, striking good looks and bright blue eyes. The more she described him the more I thought it was Kane. He was married to a young woman and had pushed Reese aside to marry her. I couldn't understand how his wife could be so young, and did some research at the library only to find he had re-married after his first wife was murdered. Reese went home, but came back, full of anger. She had been in Iraq with her husband and Kane's wife, Kelly. I'm sure you know the rest of that story, officer."

He nodded yes.

"Finally I had to tell her, that they were related! We were driving at the time. Me, Claudia, Reese and Leila… and arguing. Claudia was at the wheel… she turned to yell back at Reese and she never saw the oncoming truck. She died instantly. Leila hit her head very badly, which caused her to lose her memory. Reese and I walked away with-out a scratch." Toni started to cry as she remembered hers and Kane's child. It was too much to bear.

"Would you like to see the Commander?" the officer asked. He could arrange it.

"No. He has enough to worry about right now with his son. Is that his only son?"

"No. I believe he has three more sons and two daughters…"

She smiled through the tears. "Sounds like Kane…" She wiped her eyes. "Reese wanted a way to get back at Kane. He never wanted her, apparently. So, she took Leila with her and the child didn't know Reese wasn't her mother. Reese used her. I should have stopped her then. Gone to Kane, and told him that she was going to say the child was his. But I was scared, so I went to the convent and hid. That's where I had been working all those years and had often thought about becoming a nun. With no Leila, there was nothing to stop me. Haven't taken my vows yet… and, now, perhaps will never have the chance. Last time I heard from her, she and Boise were working on something. I don't think she told Boise everything. She just used him like she uses every-one." She looked straight at the officer's face. "If I had known what she intended to do, I would have stopped her. I really would, and Boise… he was lost to me years ago. He can be violent, like his father."

The officer sat back in the chair. She was either a damn good liar or it was all the truth. He thought the latter. "Your son is in custody for beating a cop to death… he is looking at jail time for murder." He watched her face with a trained eye.

She was telling the truth.

Kane had been inside the chapel and heard her through the thin door. He had come to do something he never did… pray. He couldn't find anything out about Hunter, so praying seemed the next best thing. He opened the door, just a little way, and stepped into the room.

"I believe you, Toni. I am sorry it all had to end this way. I wish I had known about Claudia. Whatever I can do, I will do. I will take Leila back to Sydney with me, give her a home. When the officer has taken your statements, you can return to the convent. I think you have paid a big enough price. You have lost all your children today, and losing a child is too much of a price to pay," and Kane stretched his hand down to her and held her hand just for a second. "The officer will give you a way to stay in touch with me. If you wish, you can visit your grand-daughter once in a while, or I can bring her to see you at the convent. Whatever is best for you, and for her. And, now, I must go and be with my son, and hope that I can tell this son, he has a father."

Kane closed the door and walked out into the lobby and entered a new chapter of his life.

Conclusion

"Commander Branson?" asked Dr. Pine, still dressed in scrubs. He had been looking for Kane, who had walked to the entrance doors to get air and to see if he could smoke. He couldn't.

"Yes, sir… my son… is he okay?"

"It was touch and go… he lost so much blood, but thanks to you he will recover. Would you like to see him?"

"Please. Is he conscious?" Kane was trying to hide the cigarette packet back in his pocket.

"He is not conscious yet. But you can sit with him for when he does. And no smoking in there," and Dr Pine, a veteran himself, smiled, and walked in the ER room with Kane.

The Commander thought he had never seen so many wires and tubes in all his life. It seemed to have doubled in fifteen minutes. The nurse held out a gown for Kane to pull on over his clothes and also a mask for his face. Kane mumbled something incoherent under his breath, but he donned them anyway. He sat down by the bed as close as the nursing staff would let him. He looked down at Hunter laying there, a man who never had a family, a man who was now his son. Amazing what DNA results could prove, and what havoc they could wrought. How was he going to tell the family at home about Hunter? How was he going to tell them about Leila and Claudia? He had no idea. He only knew that he had to stay here by the bed till Hunter awoke and tell him first.

"I know you can't hear me. You have always been there for me since they made you my bodyguard. My own son… ironic, really. There is so much to tell you, things about my past and things I told Sam. So much

223

catching up to do. I wish I knew who your mother was and I know you would like that, too. Maybe we can try and find her together."

Kane realized how tired he was and he leaned back in the chair. Sleep overcame him and he dozed, how long, he didn't know.

"Kane…" a very weak voice awakened him.

"Yeah, Hunter. I'm here…" and he leaned over the bed, pulling the mask from his face as he did, and leaned down on the crisp white sheets, just resting lightly on them.

"Am I going to make it?" There was a look in Hunter's eyes that Kane was surprised he had never noticed till then. Even through dark, brown eyes it was there. The same steely look as he had. How had he missed it? How had he missed the toughness of the man? Probably because he hadn't been looking for it, and now he was.

"You are going to make it, mate." Kane paused. "Hunter, maybe now is not the time, but remember I told you we had to discuss something when we got to Alice Springs?"

"Yeah, I do… you're gonna fire me, right?"

"How did you know? I am… but not for the reasons you might think."

Hunter stopped him speaking. "First, tell me… Reese?"

"The police killed her… a hail of bullets… she didn't deserve to die like she did. And before you ask, Leila is my grandchild."

"I guessed that. Now you can fire me…" and Hunter looked so sad. He didn't know what he had done to be fired.

"Remember when you had your background check when you became my bodyguard?"

"Yeah, I remember. Whole lot of crap that I didn't know what it was for," he muttered

"Hunter," and Kane glanced at the heart monitor, "Hunter, your last name is Branson. You are my son!" He watched for a reaction, his eyes once more on the monitor. It accelerated rapidly.

"What did you say? Your son… you're joking, right? I am almost the same age as Sam…"

"Yeah, I know. Seems I got around more than I thought after Nam, travelling back, stopping in towns in Australia," and Kane tried to make a joke of it and failed.

"Are you sure? I mean, this isn't a joke or something?"

"No, son. No joke. Maybe we can search for your mother. Whatever you want to do. And now you have to save your strength so we can fly you back to Sydney and tell everyone else..." This part Kane was dreading.

"Yeah... that should be fun." Hunter grimaced. It hurt, badly. "Bet you never thought you would have a son like me..."

"Makes no difference to me. Now, sleep some more... I'll be right outside... just gotta make some calls."

'Yeah,' thought Hunter, 'I'll bet you do!' "Kane? I can still call you Kane, right?"

"Sure," and Kane smiled and the smile was mirrored back at him.

"It's not going to sit well with your family..."

"Our family... and we'll deal with it... just like we did with Sam." Case closed.

Outside the room, Kane breathed a sigh of relief. One down, five to go. Buchanan already knew. Sam would be a different story, and Sage... well, she already knew her father had no morals at all... this would convince her she was right, and he thought she would probably move out, thinking the Branson mansion was no place for children to grow up in. Maybe she was right. Star... she would understand, and the boys were too young to know. Might as well do it now. Get it over with. He needed to talk to Hunter some more, but it would keep.

He called the main line into his house. Sam answered.

"Dad, where are you? Buchanan is here and he said that Reese was dead and Hunter took a bullet for you. And you found Claudia's mom? You okay?" A big babble of questions poured from Sam's mouth.

"Which do you want me to answer first? Sam, there is something you should know, and then I want you to put the phone on speaker. Is everyone there? Sage, the kids, Star?"

"Yeah, why?" But Sam had an idea why. Buchanan had been dropping hints to him all day. He whispered into the phone away from the others. "Hunter, right? He's okay? He's gonna make it?"

"Yeah, he is... why the sudden concern?" Kane was wondering.

"Because I kind of like him. He protected you with his life. That's gotta count for something..."

And Kane knew Sam had figured out he had another brother. "It's okay with you?"

"Fine, dad… Star wants to talk to you, though…"

"Put her on…" and he waited. "Baby…"

"Daddy… it's so nice to hear your voice. I miss you and I love you, daddy. Come home soon. Don't stay away any longer. I need you," she whispered down the phone. "Whatever it is, daddy, I love you and I am always right here for you," and she handed the phone back to her brother, tears in her eyes.

Now Sam switched to the speaker.

Kane composed himself, choked by his daughter's words. "Can everyone hear me," he said fairly loudly, all the while toying with the K's round his neck. "Even you Buchanan?" and Kane laughed, trying to ease the tension before it happened.

"We all hear you, loud and clear. Sage and Dan are here, the kids and Star. Sita is here, dad," replied Sam.

Kane noted that Sage did not speak to him, neither did Dan. He could hear the two youngest boys in the background teasing each other. There was only way to say it and that was outright.

"I will be coming home in a day or so as soon as Hunter can fly, and… there is something I have to tell you now, before we get there. I think Sam already figured it out." He paused. "Hunter is my son." Kane wondered if the line had been disconnected. There wasn't a sound from the other end. Then it happened, the explosion he knew would come. He could hear them yelling. "I'm still here and I can hear you all. Sage… you were right. I don't have any morals, but I will always stand by what I have done. I am not going to walk away from my responsibilities and if that doesn't suit you or anyone, that's too bad. Hunter will be coming to live with us, as will my granddaughter by a woman I didn't know was my daughter. Anyone who doesn't like it better not be there when I get back. "Star… you okay?" she was the one he was concerned about the most.

"I love you, daddy. Whatever you want is what I want." She was truly his and Kelly's daughter. The favored child.

"Thank you, baby… Sage?" and all he heard was the door slam. He had his answer. Maybe one day she would come to terms with the man he was. He nodded his head. "Sam, you there?"

"Yeah, dad… where I will always be. Seems you need two sons to keep you out of trouble, and the little ones are still little… someone has to look after them while you are a 'hired gun'," and Sam was suddenly very glad Kane was his father. "Who's the oldest, Dad?"

"You are, and you will always be my first son."

"Kane, are you okay? I mean, really okay?" Sam was concerned. This had to be stressful for his father.

"Yes, I am, son. It's just been a very long week. Please say hello to Sita for me. We'll be back in a day or two at the most. I need to go to Kelly's grave. Spend time explaining to her that she is and always will be my only love. Will you and Star go with me?"

Kane had never asked for anything in his life, and now he was.

"Do you need to ask?" and Sam felt like a new bond was forged right then and there. "Go get some rest, Kane. We'll be here waiting for you, all of us. I'll talk to Sage," and Sam hung up the line.

Kane closed the phone. There was one call left to make. He dialed, not sure if he should. He almost hoped voice mail would come on.

"Hi, it's me. Yeah, I'm still in Alice Springs. I'm probably leaving tomorrow. Flying my son back to Sydney. Hunter, yes, that son… Anyway, I'll be back up here in about a month or so if you would like to have dinner with me. Just dinner… and a glass of wine. Just as friends. No, not scotch. I'm giving that up. Seems to get me into too much trouble. You would? Great. I'll call you again nearer the time," and he closed the phone, this time for good and put it back in his boot.

And on the other end of the line 'Willowy' closed hers, also.

THE END